Close Enough
K'Barthan Extras, Hamgeean Misfit: No 3

Close Enough

K'Barthan Extras,
Hamgeean Misfit: No 3

by

M T McGuire

Hamgee University Press

First published June 2020 by
Hamgee University Press

ISBN-978-1-907809-34-7

Close Enough is written in British English with a couple of instances of light swearing. Estimated UK film rating of this book : PG (Parental Guidance).

Written by M T McGuire
Edited by Emma Wilkins
Published by Hamgee University Press
Cover design by A Trouble Halved

M T McGuire is over 50 years old now but still checks inside
unfamiliar wardrobes for a gateway to Narnia.
Boringly, she's not found any.

Thank you for buying this book.
If you enjoyed it you can keep up with
news of the author online by
visiting www.hamgee.co.uk

You can also sign up for the
M T McGuire mailing list by visiting
http://www.hamgee.co.uk/freebook
and even buy K'Barthan Series merchandise at
http://bit.ly/UHSUshop

Chapter 1
Complaints

Down in one of the posh, regenerated areas of the harbour front in Ning Dang Po, The Big Thing nightclub was packed, as usual. Most of the glitterati of the city were in tonight, and the noise from the sound system was such that even the bouncers were wearing ear plugs. Big Merv, Ning Dang Po's probably premier—and definitely most scary—gangster sat at a table in his office. With him were his two trusted deputies, Smasher Harry and Frank the Knife. Despite being soundproofed, the floor of the office space reverberated to the beat below. Big Merv liked it when the club was full like this. The atmosphere was buzzing and the bass thump reminded him of a ship's engine. It always got him in a good mood and made him feel like a pirate setting out to seek his fortune. Not that he needed to actually *seek* his fortune, per se; merely add to it. Big Merv's parents wouldn't have approved of his choice of profession, but it was one of the few that was still thriving since the Grongles invaded K'Barth.

The party mood in the club below seemed to be permeating through the floor along with the bass. The air vibrated with an electricity that filled him with energy, got his blood pumping and made him feel alive. It was why he had his office at The Big Thing, of course. Somehow he thought faster and more creatively at the club, especially when it was full. Yet at the same time, for all the lift it gave him, the vibe relaxed him, as if he was on holiday. Not that he ever had holidays. Frank and Harry were fine on their own for a day or two but they didn't have the instinct for Business that allowed them to be left in charge for any length of time. Taking too much holiday wasn't worth the hassle. It was a shame, and worse, Ms Myrtle—Big Merv's current girlfriend—liked her holidays. It was a bone of contention between the pair of them.

Still, on the bright side, Big Merv could relax in the knowledge that Frank and Harry were never going to be able to challenge his position as leader of the organisation he ran. Also, Frank and Harry were trustworthy, and the kind of deputies with the smarts to run things on their own long enough to allow Big Merv a holiday weren't. It was less stressful to pay creatures of habit like Frank and Harry who were more content to follow than lead. So long as you let them think they were helping in the decision making, and kept the wages at the right level, they were alright.

Big Merv looked at them across the desk from him, eating burgers and drinking bottled beer.

'I heard from Hal the other day,' said Frank.

'Yer?' said Big Merv. 'He done well to get word out.' Until recently, one of the main sources of income for his criminal organisation had come from his own personal discipline of choice: robbing banks. This he'd done with the help of Frank and Harry, with Hal as their driver. But then the Resistance had started funding its activities through crime and had kidnapped any half-decent getaway drivers for their extremely active Revenue Acquisition arm. Hal, the getaway man for Big Merv's gang, was one of the many who'd been forced to abandon his employer and work for them on pain of ... well, pain. Possibly even death.

'They let 'im send a birthday card to 'is mum.'

'Uncommon kind of 'em,' growled Big Merv dourly. If he'd had the resources, the Resistance wouldn't have escaped the slight of nicking his getaway man without some serious repercussions. But these days they were an organisation that not even Big Merv could confront. Not yet anyway.

'Yer. 'E reckons it ain't so bad, but the food's crap.'

'Why's that then?' asked Harry.

'No cash,' Frank shrugged.

'With all them getaway drivers? An' with all the bank jobs they done? How?' Big Merv shook his head and tutted. 'No smarts, them lot,' he said.

Big Merv was bright enough to anticipate the end of his bank-robbing days before it came. By the time the Resistance kidnapped Hal, Big Merv's organisation had already established itself in a whole host of other areas; some more legal than others. Now, a lot of the organised crime in Ning Dang Po was organised by Big Merv's firm. And anywhere where it wasn't, he was usually paid a percentage. He'd even acquired himself some legitimate investments and these, too, were thriving.

''S not the same,' said Frank.

'What ain't the same?' demanded Big Merv.

'This ...' Frank gestured to the sheet of figures on the desk in front of him. 'I miss when we was planning jobs an' that.'

'Yer, me an' all. But it ain't happenin' pal.' Big Merv heaved a sigh. These meetings had, originally, signalled the beginning of preparations for the next heist. He missed robbing banks too, but there was no point going on about it. It had been a blow initially—takings had dipped, but not as much as Big Merv expected. He'd given Frank and Harry the protection rackets to run. They clearly didn't enjoy it as much. Then again, for all the cash he was making, Big Merv didn't enjoy it as much either. 'You done well this week, lads. You got them levels of intimidation just right.'

''S no point askin' what they can't pay,' said Frank.

'Unless we wanna ice 'em,' said Harry.

'Well, yeh, that's different, innit?' agreed Frank, with a certain amount of relish.

Frank and Harry weren't as talented or as enthusiastic in Big Merv's legal business endeavours but they were very good at this. The fine burghers of the city were still paying their 'insurances' on time, and this was largely due to Frank and Harry's intimidatory skills.

On top of Frank and Harry's efforts the legitimate use of Big Merv's funds was proving to be surprisingly lucrative. Unfortunately, it was also surprisingly hard work. It required the use of good accountants and lawyers, not to mention a stockbroker, and they didn't come cheap.

Luckily, the K'Barthan Resistance had the kind of pretentions of grandeur that precluded them from sinking to extortion. They also refused to grow their funds through any investments with businesses that involved Grongles. Since that was nearly every business these days, the Resistance had ruled themselves out of pretty much any opportunity. Yeh, a bunch of stuck-up idiots, that was the Resistance, Big Merv reflected, as he pored over the sheet of figures in front of him.

''S not bad an' you boys've done good,' he said as he finished his burger, folded up the wrapper and put it to one side. 'Tell you what. I heard someone's gonna open another club down the quay.'

'What?' asked Harry. 'They got a cheek.'

'Yer,' agreed Frank. 'You want us to go round there an' smash 'em, Boss?'

'Nah! 'S plenty to go round. I got shares in it.'

'You 'ave?' asked Harry while Frank just looked crestfallen. Well, he would. He liked a good punch up, did Frank.

'Course. 'S gonna be called Ditzy's.'

Big Merv was all for a little healthy competition, so long as he had a big enough stake in all the teams involved. However, he was also aware that he seldom needed Frank and Harry to thump anyone these days, and made a mental note that he must think of something. His trusted deputies didn't enjoy all this wearing suits and behaving like one of the normals. The odd gang war from time to time was expedient to keep the lags in line.

'I reckon you could clear up one thing,' said Frank.

'Whassat?'

'The Pan of Hamgee.'

Big Merv laughed. He had to admit that, if he set Frank and Harry on The Pan of Hamgee it would keep them busy for a very long time. 'You go on an' catch the little smecker then.'

'Frank's right, Boss, you gotta use 'im or lose 'im,' said Harry.

'I gotta use 'im for the right stuff,' said Big Merv.

'Then maybe you should do more of it. Way it is now, it's like you're payin' that little scrote protection money, Boss,' said Frank.

'Nah I ain't. I'm payin' 'im coz 'e nicks less bleedin' stuff that way.'

There was a short silence while Frank and Harry did some thinking. Big Merv watched as their brows furrowed.

'Boss?' asked Harry.

'What?' said Big Merv heavily.

'What's the difference between payin' 'im so he nicks less stuff an' our customers payin' Frank an' I so we don't break stuff?' As he spoke, Harry, sprayed burger crumbs across the table. Big Merv gave him a bit of a look. 'Sorry Boss.'

'There's a lotta difference.'

'How, Boss?'

'Coz it ain't the same,' said Big Merv.

'Why?'

'Coz he don't *always* nick stuff.'

'He smeckin' does, Boss!' said Frank.

'Alright, some. But he blags a lot, you know— does odd jobs for food an' that.'

'No, he don't!' said Frank.

'Nah, the boss is right, Frank, he does,' said Harry. 'Problem is he does them so crap. Arnold's conkers,' he laughed, 'you should see 'im trying DIY. Mrs Minton up Rossiter Street had 'im puttin' up shelves. Word is he done such a rubbish job she gave 'im half a dozen eggs to go away.'

Frank started snickering.

'Yer, I get that The Pan of Hamgee's a liability,' said Big Merv. 'Thing is though lads, the little nerk makes the effort. He only nicks a bit of stuff here an' there to stay alive.'

'So? Our customers *pay* us to stay alive.'

'They think. But, they pays us to stay *in business* and that's a whole different score. Listen boys, the best thing about chucking a couple of bad 'uns into the river from time to time is that all we gotta do is make sure a few folks know an' everyone toes the line.'

Frank thought for a moment. 'OK, Boss, so we make it look like we're gonna do it more often than we does but so what? That still don't answer my question. Why that little nerk?'

'Coz he's only a kid an' if he don't nick food or blankets, or break into some geezer's lock-up to spend the night, he dies. Our customers, we never ask 'em to pay more than they can afford to pay us. That kid? He's givin' us all he's got. He's just survivin'.'

'Then we tell 'im to go survive somewhere else, don't we?'

'Nah,' said Big Merv. ''S collateral damage, teethin' problems, this nickin' stuff.'

'You what, Boss?'

'There's a place for that spotty little numpty in my

organisation. Thing is, right now, ain't one hundred percent certain what it is, see? So I gotta experiment while I suss that out.'

'You sure? Only, if he crosses yer, no-one's gonna catch him,' said Harry.

'Exactly. No-one ever catches that little nerk, so nobody disrupts my deliveries. That's why he does the personal stuff. That an' he's a well brought-up lad; polite, makes a good impression. Ms Myrtle likes 'im a lot, an' she's a pukka judge of character.'

'He ain't polite, Boss. He's scared of you.'

Big Merv shrugged, 'Same difference to the end user, innit?'

'Fists reckons he's on the blacklist,' said Frank.

'Makes 'im risky, donnit?' agreed Harry.

Big Merv shrugged. 'I reckon Fists could be right. Course, if the little Herbert *is* a GBI he'll be dead in a few weeks an' we ain't got nothing to worry about.'

'There's hundreds of starvin' kids what you could help. Why 'im?' asked Harry.

'Yer,' agreed Frank. 'Look, Boss, if you gotta help some little git why not go the whole hog? Pay 'im proper, so he don't have to nick nothing?'

Big Merv heaved a sigh. The Pan of Hamgee was smart and resourceful. He liked that in the lad.

'An' while you're at it, why not find one what folks can trust?'

'One you like, you mean,' growled Big Merv.

Frank scratched his head.

'C'mon boys. Ain't you seen what happens around that lad?' asked Big Merv.

'What, people gettin' pissed off an' trying to slot 'im?' asked Frank. 'Folks love 'im or loathe 'im.'

'I get that lads, an' I get that you loathe 'im. I mean the

folks what *do* like 'im. That's how he's still around. Them old ladies down that pub, an' all them punters. They got the whole of Turnadot Street lookin' out for 'im. He don't know it of course; he ain't got no confidence so he's not gonna work nothing like that out. Not yet. But there's something about that little numpty what makes a lotta hard cases get soft. An' I wanna know what it is, coz I reckon it's something I can use. Arnold's cobblers, even *I* get soft round 'im.'

'Yer Boss. That's what we're sayin'. We reckon—'

'Indulge me boys. Call the little bleeder a charity project. It's gonna pay us back, this. Karma. I'll bet my cobblers on that. Coz if a lot of people like the little toe rag, and we look out for him, that's a lotta people who are gonna like us an' all. How d'you think I got to be the boss?'

'You smashed everyone what got in your way?'

Big Merv's antennae wiggled from side to side. ''S a fair point but it's not what I'm talking about.'

'People are scared of you, Boss?'

'Nah. Well, yer, but it's about trust an' all, lads. It don't matter how scared folks are of me—they know I'm fair an' honourable. I ain't gonna ask for nothing what they can't give. It might be hard for 'em but they can still give it. An' they know they'll get the respect they deserve. If something goes down an' I have to have a word, they know they'll get a fair hearing, even if I do ice a few of 'em after. They *trust* me lads, that's what I'm sayin'. And a lotta folks trust 'im.'

Big Merv sighed heavily. It was difficult to explain to Frank and Harry what he saw in The Pan of Hamgee, but he was beginning to suspect it was himself. As a young Thing arriving in Ning Dang Po without a penny in his pocket, Big Merv knew he'd probably have sunk without trace were it not for the intervention of the (then) boss of the city, Abraham the Awful. Abraham had been far less awful than folklore made out. He'd taken on Big Merv as an errand boy first, then as a problem solver. Big Merv had solved a lot of Abraham the Awful's problems. However, unlike his predecessor in the job, he'd managed to do so with the minimum of bloodshed. Big Merv quickly understood that nobody wanted an out-and-out gang war. Few organisations could withstand such a loss of earnings and staff. A smooth operation was ten percent strong arm and about ninety percent staff training, job satisfaction and negotiation skills. Big Merv had learned how to negotiate and how to run a 'business' from within one of the best. More importantly he learned the value, the true value, of a life.

When Abraham the Awful finally died at the ripe old age of eighty three, there'd been a period of gangland anarchy in Ning Dang Po. At the end of it, thanks to what Abraham had taught him, and some things he'd learned for himself, Big Merv had built up a sizeable organisation of his own. These days, Big Merv ran a lot of the city. And if he didn't run it, he earned a nice fat commission from the people who did.

The Pan of Hamgee had brains and tact. That was a lot of potential, if the little scrote could just man up and learn to rein in his big mouth. Yeh, He might turn out to be a useful asset. Or Frank and Harry might be right, and Big Merv might end up chucking him in the river Dang. It was too early to tell just yet.

Still, Big Merv thought to himself, this sort of stuff wasn't the kind of thing Frank and Harry would understand. No, it was probably prudent to give the little Hamgeean scrote a job to do. He didn't want any unrest in his organisation because the lads were thinking he'd gone soft. Yeh, and he reckoned he knew just the thing.

Chapter 2
A new job

The Pan of Hamgee was feeling chipper. Having earned some cash he'd given it to Gerry, who was officially Work Experience Creature at the Great Snurd (of K'Barth) Company Limited, but unofficially the best mechanic they had, for some repairs to his wheels. When he arrived it was still early, because people who are sleeping on the streets get cold and wake up early, even if, technically it wasn't the streets because The Pan had slept in someone's heated greenhouse.

Despite the early hour, Gerry was already at work and busy with another customer. While The Pan waited for him to finish he wandered around the line of vehicles which were repaired and awaiting collection. At the end was an immaculate snurd. It was a midnight-blue, sleek four-seater. Far away, in another version of the universe it was a MKII Jaguar. Here in K'Barth it was a snurd MKII. The Pan watched the mechanics fussing round it, buffing and polishing it to a factory-fresh shine. He recognised it as Big Merv's.

'Very nice,' he said when Gerry arrived.

'Yeh, in your dreams,' he answered, punching The Pan playfully on the arm. 'Come on, let's go into the workshop and I'll give you the lowdown on yours.'

As a Blaggysomp, one of the mountain species of K'Barth, a ring of blue fluff stuck out from Gerry's collar and cuffs betraying the presence of a luxuriant coat of blue fur underneath. He tugged at his ear with one hand and fixed The Pan with an apologetic expression. 'Aw mate, I'm sorry. I've got bad news.'

'Please don't tell me it's terminal,' said The Pan, fearful that he was going to be told his beloved snurd was good for nothing but scrap.

Gerry laughed. 'What are you like? You don't half get melodramatic about things. This one will run and run, mate. Whether it'll run reliably is a whole different question, but it's going to run, and when I'm done, it'll run good. No, we had a rush job in. My boss insisted and I couldn't get yours finished.'

'That's OK,' said The Pan.

'Should be done by supper time: if not sooner. I'm just sorry it isn't finished now. I came in early and I was sure I'd get it sorted but ...' he shrugged and then proceeded to go into lengthy technical detail about some important bits which had seized together and had to be coaxed apart with copious amounts of time, patience and three-in-one oil. 'Next time we'll book it in for two days, then you'll know where you're at and I won't be messing you around.'

'No worries. If you have trouble again, you can leave me a message at The Parrot and Screwdriver,' said The Pan, hoping desperately that Gladys, Ada and Their Trev wouldn't mind. 'It's on Turnadot Street.'

The Pan watched Gerry trying not to show what he thought of Turnadot Street as he wrote down the address. Well, The Pan conceded, it was a bit of a hole, but he fitted in and they were good beings down there. He thought of the punters at The Parrot, most of whom earned their living by committing felonies of some description. OK, so probably not 'good' exactly, but they were loyal (after a fashion) they accepted him as he was and they didn't ask him any awkward questions.

'Shall I give the pub a bell when it's done then, yeh?'

'Yes please. If you leave the spare keys under the seat and park it somewhere it can escape, I'll just summon it when I hear from you.' One of the joys of The Pan's ancient vehicle was that, for all its clapped-out nature, it had once been a luxury item. That meant it came with homing and self park, so all The Pan had to do when he wanted to use it was press a button on the key ring and it would come to him. Likewise, when he reached his destination, a press of the same button and it would go and park itself. Both these were premium options, but it also had some other very non-standard extras, like a revolving number plate.

'Righty tighty, willco,' said Gerry.

The Pan's snurd had been designed in an era when vehicles were all round edges and sweeping curves. Despite its age, it still looked futuristic, in a retrotastic kind of way. He looked at it, sitting supreme, and possibly a little smug, in the corner of the workshop at the centre of a sea of Gerry's tools. 'Sorry it's been so tricky, Gerry.'

'It's always tricky, but whoever built this one really knew his stuff. I wouldn't wonder if it was old man Snurd himself. I know it's a bit clapped out now but it's golden, and when I get it running right, it'll be a peach. Don't worry, I'll have it fixed today. I'll ring the pub, like you asked, when it's done.'

'Thanks Gerry. See you later.'

They shook hands and then, as The Pan stepped out of the Great Snurd (of K'Barth) Company Limited's workshop and onto the street, a voice called his name. He stopped and realised it was Bob, who sometimes chauffeured Big Merv.

Despite her name, Bob was a lady, and when she wasn't driving Big Merv around, she worked behind the bar in The Big Thing, the night club Big Merv owned. As a more benign and motherly member of Big Merv's organisation, she tended to be the one who liaised with The Pan about his delivery jobs. Like Gerry, Bob was also a Blaggysomp. 'Hi Bob,' said The Pan.

'Thought I'd find you here. Gerry said you were coming in. I just come to collect Big Merv's wheels.'

'I was ogling those a few minutes ago,' said The Pan.

Bob chuckled. 'Yer, can't say I mind driving them.'

Big Merv's MKII snurd was legendary. It came with every conceivable add-on and was an identikit of the getaway vehicle used by the Mervinettes, the gang of bank robbers which Big Merv led, even if officially he had nothing to do with them and a cast-iron alibi for the duration of every robbery. Unofficially, everyone who was anyone among a certain kind of underclass knew the Mervinettes were Big Merv's gang and that this was the getaway vehicle they used.

'You want a lift back to town?' asked Bob as one of Gerry's fellow mechanics parked the MKII beside them and handed over the keys.

'If you're going that way, just drop me around Turnadot Street somewhere.'

'Hop in then. I'm glad I found you,' Bob continued as the snurd pulled away, 'the boss wanted me to give you this. I was supposed to deliver it to that pub you more-or-less live at, but seeing as you're here ... Hang on.' She riffled about in the glove compartment as she drove, which The Pan found slightly alarming, in case it interfered with her concentration. But she kept the snurd steering straight and true as she rummaged, and finally produced an envelope. 'Here you go.' The Pan took it. 'You going to open it?'

'In a while,' he sighed. 'In a while.'

Since The Pan had been a regular at The Parrot and Screwdriver, he'd begun to get to know the area in which it was situated. There was a coffee house nearby, on the corner of Dumpty Street and Market Square—Mama Jack's it was called. Mama Jack's daughter ran it now, so in theory it was really Jenny Jack's, but she'd never changed the name. She'd been an acrobat until she'd injured her shoulder and it became too painful to do backflips night after night. These days her injury still lingered and she found it painful wiping the tables down. So if The Pan turned up early and offered to do them for her, she'd usually give him breakfast in return for his trouble. It was strange how even the tiny retainer he received from Big Merv allowed him space to plan, to think ahead, and find alternative ways to feed and clothe himself instead of just nicking stuff.

Maybe he was getting to know people around the city, or maybe he'd just been around long enough to convince anyone who thought he was on the blacklist that he was kosher after all. Little did they know. Even The Pan couldn't believe how long he'd lasted sometimes, since he was on the blacklist and his existence was illegal. Of course, it could be that he was becoming known as an employee of Big Merv. Even if it wasn't, he was grateful to Big Merv for the time the tiny retainer he paid bought.

The Grongles had started to relax a bit these days too. Maybe they had other, easier prey to chase. Or were there more places where the management were willing to let The Pan help out in return for a meal? Or was that the confidence thing? Was he just less afraid to ask? He couldn't be certain. Whatever it was, anything that reduced the number of irate beings looking for him was OK. 'Every cloud has a silver lining,' he muttered.

'Say what?' said Bob.

'Sorry, talking to myself.'

'You won't forget to open that, will you?'

'No, Mum,' said The Pan. 'But if it's another delivery, I'd rather eat first and read it on a full stomach. How's Mr Bob and the kids?'

'Peachy, sweetheart, just peachy. We're nearly at Turnadot Street. Where shall I drop you?'

'Mama Jack's please.' The early morning rush had begun and the traffic was building. Dumpty Street was reduced to a slow crawl. Bob and The Pan chatted about this and that, and eventually, he decided he may as well open the letter. 'Arnold's trollies! Does it have to be today?'

'If that's what he says sweetheart, yes, it does.'

'Marvellous. Tomorrow I'll have wheels, but today they're still at Snurd. And I don't like the idea of collecting anything from a jeweller's shop on foot. Especially at eleven o'clock in the morning.'

'That when you have to go get it?'

'Yeh. Then I have to deliver it to Big Merv's girlfriend, up at their place in The Planes, at eight.'

'Ooo, well posh,' said Bob. 'At least you'll be alright up there. Nobody gets mugged in The Planes—it's far too smart.'

'True, but I'm not. I'll have to be careful not to get myself arrested. That said, strangely, I'm not too concerned about that. I've been to The Planes before. Nope, it's the rest of the day I'm worried about.'

'Which shop d'you have to collect it from?'

'Flynn and Flynn on Tarbot Street.'

'Finicky Bert's? You'll be alright there, son, he's a lovely geezer. Used to be a trapeze artist. One of the best apparently.'

'Really? That's ... quite a career change.'

'Nah, he were always a jeweller too—makes some of the best stuff in the city. He's just properly into the circus and he liked a little bit of adventure, I guess. You know, before he settled down, like. Probably like yerself.' The Pan left Bob's invitation to talk about himself unanswered. 'Times like this I wish the boss would let me use aviator,' said Bob waving a hand at the button on the dash marked 'wings'.

'He doesn't?' asked The Pan.

'Nah, he's a nervous flier.'

'He's not here. Why would he care if you used it now?'

'I wish I knew,' said Bob, 'But it's no-go. I expect I could get away with it but knowing my luck, I'd get seen by someone. Big Merv has a way of finding out stuff.'

'Yeh,' agreed The Pan. Didn't he just?

Chapter 3
The pick up

The Pan had cleaned the skirting boards at Mama Jack's as well as the tables, and for this, Jenny Jack had declared herself eternally grateful. Grateful enough to give him an extra large breakfast comprising proper fresh coffee and scrambled eggs. He arrived on Tarbot Street with a spring in his step, albeit a slightly burpy one. He was twenty minutes early to give himself time to have a quick recce, and as he walked the length of Tarbot Street he soon identified Flynn and Flynn.

The street was a small one and fed onto another road which was simply called Outgate. It had once been a main route out of Ning Dang Po, and was in an area of the city The Pan didn't often frequent. This part of town had been gentrified a couple of hundred years before when some beings of means began to move out of the city centre and live in newly built grand houses in the suburbs. Outgate was a classic example of one of these neighbourhoods; all wide, tree-lined streets and houses of pale golden bricks with porticos, tall windows and high-ceilinged rooms. But now there were ragged stumps where the trees had been, the windows were cracked and boarded up, the brickwork was black, not gold, and most of the grand houses had several families living in them.

Even in its heyday, Tarbot Street had never been as smart as Outgate once was. The buildings were smaller and much more of a mix. Some were several centuries older than those on Outgate itself. Then again, Tarbot Quay had been in use for hundreds of years before the gentrification of

Outgate. Perhaps Tarbot Street was part of the original settlement. Tarbot was a suburb now but it had been a separate town when the quay was first built. Presumably its proximity to the river, and the canal once that was constructed, had meant the air got a bit fruity come summer. That was probably why the gentrified houses were on Outgate, just that little bit further away. 'Out of range of the smell,' The Pan muttered to himself.

A lot of the Tarbot Street houses were timber framed. But while some were incredibly ornate, others were rudimentary—primitive almost. The Pan guessed that these were built for the workers on the quays nearby and decided that the more ornate ones were probably owned by the foremen or perhaps even merchants, as they earned their way up the property ladder to the luxurious mansions on Outgate. Other Tarbot Street properties had been places of trade. Statues and carvings on the walls and wooden beams denoted the goods originally sold there: fish, meat, cloth—standard fare for the times in which they were built. Dotted in among them were more modern shops, or at least, shops that were contemporary with the buildings on Outgate rather than the majority of the ones on Tarbot Street.

Flynn and Flynn was a typical example of one of the old shops. The door was set in the centre, three feet or so back from the pavement, and huge glass-paned front windows curved inwards either side of it. Windows like that would have been expensive, The Pan thought. Clearly the monied folk on nearby Outgate had come to visit the shops on Tarbot Street in days gone by, even if they hadn't stooped to live there.

The Pan was glad that Turnadot Street wasn't that far away. If it *was* actually jewellery he was collecting from Flynn and Flynn, the best course of action might be to take it straight to The Parrot and Screwdriver. He could ask Gladys and Ada to hide it behind the bar until the time came when he was supposed to deliver it to The Planes. Meanwhile, he was still early. So he walked up the street to the end and back down to the jeweller's again.

The jewellery in the window was mostly mid-priced, mass-produced stuff: pieces in a common style. Gold coins made into knuckle duster rings for the kinds of beings who worked for Big Merv, chains and bangles for their wrists, and blingy baubles or trinkets for their ladies.

As The Pan walked past the jeweller's shop a third time, an elderly shop assistant in a jacket and waistcoat who'd been arranging the window display stopped work to consult a pocket watch. Spotting The Pan, he beckoned to him to come in.

The door was a little stiff and had a bell which tinkled tinnily, both when The Pan opened it and when he pushed it closed. The inside of the shop smelled like old books and furniture polish, with a dash of coffee and the merest hint of burned toast. The assistant, or maybe he was the owner, walked forward to greet The Pan.

'Good morning,' the old boy said as he stuffed the watch into a pocket in his waistcoat and extended his hand. 'I'm Bert Stipplethwaite.'

'Finicky Bert?'

'The same.' They shook hands. There was a slight pause. 'Are you here for ...?' Finicky Bert tailed off.

'I have a package to collect for my boss, Big Merv.'

'I must commend you on your excellent timekeeping.' Finicky Bert looked The Pan up and down. 'You're not quite what I was expecting.' The Pan raised an eyebrow. 'It's no good looking at me like that. You're no thug. And you can't pretend you're a cold-blooded killer either. If this was a circus you'd be with the clowns.'

The Pan held his hands out either side of him in a suitably theatrical Hamgeean shrug. 'You probably have me there.'

'Yes. Unmistakeable clown. Some of the fastest and fittest people in the circus are the clowns, and they're usually the smartest and most adaptable. I'd say you're a bit of a diplomat, too.'

The Pan flashed him a rueful smile. 'Judging by the amount of trouble I get myself into, I suspect I'm not.'

'Perhaps, without those diplomatic skills, you'd get yourself into more.'

The Pan wondered if that was actually possible. Mmm ... maybe. He shrugged. 'That's ... a lot more complimentary than I expected. But I think you flatter me. I'm just a messenger boy.'

Finicky Bert winked. 'And a clown, remember,' he said. 'Everyone loves a clown.'

I'm not sure they do, thought The Pan as a mental image of Harry and Frank popped into his head.

'It's a reflection of life, the circus, which is why, after all these years, it's still so successful,' Bert added.

'I see.' The Pan scratched his head. This was all a bit odd. He should probably just pick up the box and be on his way. On the other hand, he didn't want to come across as rude. Finicky Bert was clearly a decent old cove, even if he was a bit eccentric, and as one of Big Merv's connections, making a good impression on him counted. Bob had said that Finicky Bert was once a trapeze artist. Looking at him, it made sense. The old boy was small and slight, but there was a wiriness and athleticism about him.

'As a way of categorising beings, the circus can't be bettered,' Finicky Bert was saying.

Well, The Pan supposed, everyone made sense of life by putting the folks around them into boxes and everyone did that in their own particular manner. Bert's method wasn't that much weirder than any other he'd encountered. 'So who are you, then, in the circus line-up?' he asked.

'Trapeze artist, of course. Ahhhh.' Bert's eyes misted over. 'Even now, the smell of the chalk, the excitement, the finesse, the beauty and accuracy of the discipline ... The trapeze is its own small wonder. You have to have amazing powers of retention and attention to detail. You have to train doggedly. If you perform with a partner you have to learn to anticipate them by instinct, as if they were you. It translates poorly to other areas of course. I have a narrow field of operations now, and it's jewellery. You want anything in my field, I'm your man. If you want me to adapt, or do something else alongside, you dismiss me from the job and call a clown. A clown can always be trusted to think on his feet.'

'So what does that make Big Merv?'

'What do you think?'

'I'm tempted to say ringmaster, but I think he's probably the impresario pulling the strings, making us marionettes move.'

'That's a very interesting guess, and it says a lot about you, but you're wrong.'

The Pan thought for a moment. 'You have him down as another clown then, do you?'

'Of course! He may well be the impresario now but he's a clown at heart. Perhaps that's what he sees in you.' The Pan cleared his throat politely and the old boy stopped short. 'Sorry, what am I doing, banging on at you like this? You must think I'm absolutely batty.'

The Pan said nothing because that was exactly what he thought.

'I spent many years on the trapeze as a younger, more vigorous man,' Finicky Bert added.

'One of my colleagues mentioned that. If you were a jeweller at the same time, doesn't that make you a clown?'

'Oh no. Jewellery was always my metier. I studied the trapeze, but I was never very good. I was more of an enthusiastic fan.'

'My colleague said you were very good.'

'They flatter me.'

'It must have been a very interesting life,' said The Pan.

'It was hard, but the beings performing with me, they were good folks and they were fascinating.'

'I can imagine you have some stories,' said The Pan.

'That I do, but we'll have to leave those for next time,' said Finicky Bert.

The Pan was surprised. He had, at the least, expected to hear a tale or two and felt that, somehow, he'd missed an opportunity, or, perhaps, asked the wrong question. Although he wasn't sure what he should have asked. Then again, maybe it was just because the old boy knew that The Pan worked for Big Merv and didn't want to take up too much of his time.

'Now,' Finicky Bert held up one finger, 'if you'll just wait a moment.' He went behind the counter. The Pan watched him bend down, out of sight, and listened to the sound of a drawer opening. Then the old boy put a dark blue leather-covered box on the counter top. 'Here we are.'

Suddenly there was a focus and an incisiveness to Finicky Bert that hadn't been there before. Perhaps he'd called time on expanding on his enthusiasm about the circus to indulge a greater passion. The old fellow opened the box with a theatrical flourish and The Pan's eyes goggled. 'These are made as per Big Merv's remit. I hope they'll be suitable.'

Nestling in special, bespoke-fitted indentations in the midnight-blue velvet lining of the box lay a pair of sapphire and diamond earrings. Delicate, surprisingly tasteful and un-blingy, the stones caught the light, reflecting rainbow patterns on Fincky Bert's face and eyebrows. The Pan was no expert but they looked premium quality to him. He whistled before he could stop himself. 'Blimey. They look as if they should be in a museum.'

'Hardly. They're a modern copy of an older style.'

'Did you make them?'

'Of course.'

'They're wonderful.'

'Only the best for Big Merv, eh?'

'Uh ... yeh.' The Pan swallowed. He wasn't supposed to be delivering the earrings until the evening. But he definitely didn't fancy wandering around Ning Dang Po all day with those on board. No, he'd go straight to The Parrot and Screwdriver, and ask Gladys and Ada to hide them behind the bar.

'Shall I wrap them for you?'

Had Big Merv said anything about gift wrapping? No. 'They're fine as is, thanks.'

Chapter 4
Unfortunate encounter

The Pan stepped out of the jewellers into the watery sunshine. It was still cold but there was a scent of promise in the air that hinted at spring. He felt the weight of the box Big Merv had asked him to collect; or, at least, the weight of the responsibility. What was it The Big Thing had said he'd be delivering when he hired The Pan? Trinkets? Information? The sapphire earrings in the box were a bit more than trinkets—understated and elegant, they seemed to scream quality in the way that only something made by a true craftsman can.

Ideally, The Pan would use his wheels for a job like this, especially after such a large breakfast at Mama Jack's. However, since the snurd was still with Gerry, in pieces, The Pan had no choice but to start walking. Maybe he was a bit sluggish after all those scrambled eggs, or perhaps his nervousness was interfering with his powers of observation. Whatever it was, as he made his way along the street, he suddenly came face to face with Killer Mike, a butcher who ran a stall at a market away out on the edge of town in Upper Right. Killer Mike was notable to The Pan simply because the meat stall he ran was on The Pan's rota of 'suppliers', as in it was one of the many places he attempted to blag food from, on strict rotation so that none of them saw him more than a couple of times every few months.

Unfortunately, the previous morning it had been Killer Mike's turn on the roster and The Pan had relieved him of a meat pie. In The Pan's defence, he'd volunteered to work for food. Then, after spending a morning flogging second-rate pies with what he felt was skill and aplomb, not to mention a degree of success, Killer Mike had changed his mind. When asked for payment, he refused to give so much as a crust. The Pan had argued but Killer Mike was an extremely large gentleman, whereas The Pan was not. Killer Mike was also armed with a meat cleaver at the time, and The Pan was not. But despite those strong deterrents, feeling bullied and taken advantage of, and somewhat uppity about it, The Pan had grabbed a chicken pie and legged it.

Now here he was, face to face with Killer Mike outside a smart jeweller's. It might have been slightly better if the pie had been worth nicking. Killer Mike's face went through several shades of pink and purple to full-on puce, his eyes popped and his mouth set into an angry snarl. He held up one hand, finger extended. But before he'd even uttered the word 'You!', The Pan turned and fled. As he did so, Mike managed to shout, 'Stop thief!'

It being a busy street, and this exchange taking place outside a jeweller's, the beings nearby assumed that The Pan had stolen some actual jewellery. As a result they took Killer Mike's shout a lot more seriously than they might have done if they'd known the item nicked was actually a three-zloty chicken pie, especially one which contained a very small quantity of meat that probably wasn't chicken anyway. A likely lad coming towards The Pan put his foot out. The Pan jumped, but the thug knew about that and lifted the foot higher, catching The Pan's shins and sending him sprawling on the pavement.

Arse.

Both the likely lad and Killer Mike made a lunge to grab him but The Pan was up and running, albeit with the pursuit extremely close behind.

'Stop thief!' Killer Mike shouted again as the two of them ran after him.

Marvellous, thanks Mike! thought The Pan as what felt like the entire street full of people joined the chase. He ducked and dived over a variety of beings coming at him from all sides. Arnold's bottom! The security forces would be getting involved any minute. This was not good. The pursuit was too close for The Pan to head for the roofs; he didn't have time for the momentary pause required to grab a drainpipe and start to climb. It was a pity because taking the chase to roofs, leaping from building to building, tended to separate the men from the boys. And in many cases, the pursuit from The Pan.

Nothing for it but to keep running. He skidded down an alley which exited onto the towpath along the canal. Accelerating across the muddy gravel he leapt onto the roof of a passing longboat, skipped over another that was making its way along the canal in the opposite direction, onto the roof of a third moored on the other side, and onto the opposite path. There was a shout and a loud splash as some of the pursuit tried to follow him but misjudged it and fell in.

Excellent, that had extended his lead. But now there were no scalable walls. There was no way off the towpath here either. The canal on one side and the tall sides of the warehouses on the other hemmed him in. And although they hadn't yet jumped the canal, the pursuit was already making for a bridge a few hundred yards up.

The Pan headed for Tarbot Quay. Just behind it was Tarbot Square which had a small market. The area had suffered in the invasion but these days, among the (mostly) deserted warehouses was the occasional one which looked a little cleaner and more cared for. New businesses were beginning to move in. Tarbot was still a rough area though, where people were pinched and mean, and, more to the point, streetwise. They would know what The Pan was about the minute they saw him because most of them were living on the breadline like he was. That could go one of two ways—they might see him with sympathy, as an equal, the way the community round Turnadot Street did. Or they might see him as unwelcome competition. He hoped it would be the former.

The Pan didn't know anyone in Tarbot. It was the kind of place where he didn't even try to work in exchange for food. Life was that hard that few had enough for themselves, let alone anyone else, and The Pan felt it was wrong to ask anyone to spare any.

On the upside, the fact that nobody there knew him would be an advantage. And with any luck, poor area or not, the market would be busy and The Pan could get lost among the shoppers. Even if he couldn't, at least the throng of beings would hamper Killer Mike and his newfound friends.

The Pan finally reached an exit from the towpath, skidded round a corner and found himself in the marketplace. He was beginning to tire and his pursuers were hot on his tail again, when a man pulling a large cart full of apples moved slap bang into his path. The Pan leapt, dived over the top of it and rolled into a small gap between a gaggle of Spiffles inspecting some cooking implements and a group of hard-faced men looking at tools. Before any of them could react he ran on. He heard a crash behind him as Killer Mike hit the cart at full speed and it toppled over, apples tumbling everywhere.

Smeck. Why did stuff like this always have to happen? He'd have to find a way to make it up to that apple seller.

'Oi!' shouted someone as Killer Mike, and what was now a large group, thundered after The Pan, crushing apples underfoot.

'Stop thief!' shouted Killer Mike again, but the extra

burst of adrenaline from leaping over the cart had given The Pan's tired legs a new lease of life. He was accelerating away now.

He slid through a gap between two stalls and ducked into a small side street lined with more. They were set up on trestle tables with sacking and canvas cloths over them. The usual wares were on display; second-hand shoes, fruit, home-grown vegetables and 'valuables' picked up at bomb sites or stolen from the unwary. The obvious place to hide was under the drapes on one of the stalls. So instead The Pan ducked into an open doorway as if he was just popping into his own house. It lead into a passageway, which he walked briskly down as if he had every business to be there. It was a tenement and along the passage he passed dirty malnourished youths of various species lounging in doorways.

Beyond, to his disappointment was a yard. Immediately, The Pan sensed trouble. As he stood in the middle and turned in a circle he realised the place was deserted—no kids playing football for example. A basket of damp laundry stood on the ground next to a washing line, half of it pegged out, the owner nowhere in evidence.

Arnold's toe jam! How could I be such an idiot? he thought. Yes. Something was definitely 'about to go down,' as Big Merv would have put it. Time for a swift exit.

Except there was no way out other than the way he'd come in. Sheer walls stretched up five storeys all around him. Sure, there were windows and doors but they were tightly closed. There was also a drainpipe but The Pan doubted it was secure enough to take his weight long enough to reach the roof. And there were no obvious handholds near it.

Ah, but wait. Just next to the entrance through which he'd come there was an outside staircase. However, no sooner had he noticed it when he realised it was blocked by a group of unfriendly looking males, mostly humans.

Arnold's sweaty armpits! Not a gang.

Yes, a gang. And worse, whatever was going down was happening on those stairs. Indeed, it was clear the gang was in the middle of whatever business it was that everyone had left the area to avoid. From the looks of it, they were kicking the living daylights out of some poor blighter. OK, so they were there, and that was bad, but they were busy and they hadn't seen him yet.

Time to go.

As The Pan started back to the passageway and the exit, Killer Mike and the rest of his mob spilled out of it into the yard. 'Arnold's pants,' muttered The Pan.

OK, maybe the drainpipe was a better option. He took a cautious step back. Killer Mike took a step forward and his helpers fanned out either side of him. Schoolboy error on their part. The Pan felt the first flutterings of hope.

He took another step back and Killer Mike, plus posse, started to walk forward. Please Arnold, let them keep coming.

Killer Mike appeared to have helped himself to a hammer from somewhere and the expression of thunderous rage on his face suggested that he intended to use it. For the first time, it dawned on The Pan that maybe, just maybe, Killer Mike's nickname was not to do with his size and temper but had been earned literally. There was a grim thought. Using the useful extra pair of eyes in the back of his head, The Pan checked behind him. The square was deserted. A few yards away was the dodgy drainpipe he'd considered using. Looking at it now, it definitely wasn't an option. Neither were the locked front doors of each of the single-room ground floor apartments.

However, as The Pan's gaze lit on the row of windows

along the wall at just about waist height, he had an idea. He kept walking slowly backwards while Killer Mike and his crew, without breaking formation, kept pace. A couple of feet short of the window, The Pan stopped.

'Finally, I've caught up with you, you little smeck,' said Killer Mike.

'Can we talk about this?'

'You stole from me.'

'No, I didn't.' The Pan eyed the hammer. He knew it was bad to steal and he probably deserved a good kicking but Arnold's bottom! It wasn't as if he'd taken a bit of prime steak, or even some sausages. It was only a pie and the meat in it ... well, The Pan could imagine that the area around Killer Mike's premises was mysteriously free of cats and dogs, or any other stray fauna.

'When people steal from me, they pay,' said Killer Mike.

'I did a morning's work.'

'No, you didn't, you lazy little shazzbutt! You sat on your arse! You didn't sell a thing!'

'I tried though! Anyway, it'd take the best salesman on earth to flog any of those pies. I know, I ate one.'

'Why you little—' Killer Mike lifted the hammer high and lunged.

The Pan turned and leapt upwards. Putting one foot on a windowsill, he flipped himself over Killer Mike's head and landed behind him. He was halfway across the yard accelerating towards the exit before Killer Mike had even turned round. But The Pan had momentarily forgotten about the gang on the stairs. Clearly they'd finished whatever it was they were doing and decided to help Mike catch him.

The Pan dodged a huge and lumbering bloke who was so covered in muscles he looked more like a ball of living gristle than a man, and ducked two flying Blurpons. Then, as he jinked right to avoid some guy coming in from the left, another stepped in from the right, swinging his arm up in a high tackle across The Pan's neck and taking him down with apparently little effort. He felt his legs come out from under him, then he slammed onto the concrete and for a moment everything went black.

Chapter 5
Disaster

'Get him up,' said a voice. The Pan felt arms haul him upward. The back of his head was throbbing as he tried to gather his scattered thoughts. Oh yeh, that's right—Killer Mike, and now this bloke. His vision was a bit blurry, so he closed his eyes to let it settle. Someone picked up his hat and jammed it on his lolling head. Despite the apparent helpfulness of this gesture it didn't feel like a good sign, or kindly meant. His shoulders were aching, but The Pan realised this was because he appeared to be hanging, limp-kneed, rather than standing. Was someone holding him up? Yes. With a bit of cajoling he managed to persuade his legs to hold him upright, and the pain in his shoulders abated a little as they took his weight. Unfortunately his head was still throbbing big time, but his mind was gaining focus. He opened his eyes but didn't dare open the secret pair in the back of his head. He could feel the breath of the person holding his arms on the back of his neck—if the fellow was that close, there was a chance he might notice them. Things were a bit blurry to start with but slowly, his vision cleared.

Standing in front of him was not a bloke, but a human female. She wore leather trousers and a waistcoat, with a baggy white shirt underneath. The shirt was undone enough to give a tantalising glimpse of her breasts. Noooo, Arnold in the skies don't look at her cleavage! She also had an impressive collection of scars. Her sleeves were rolled up to show off the gang tattoos on her forearms and she was clearly fight-fit, rather than gym-fit. She was attractive but haughty with it, her light blue eyes cold, her face hard and cruel. She was wearing a leather bandana over black hair in a series of long plaits, like the arms of an octopus.

Uh-oh, thought The Pan.

Her companions wore a similar uniform—leather trousers and open shirts, or no shirt at all and tattoos, except for the two Blurpon members who were too furry for tattoos and, rather than clothes, wore long bandoliers bristling with weaponry. In fact all of them were armed to the teeth, but it was the armaments of the street: chains, knives, hammers and in one case, a lump of wood. The leader, the one currently in The Pan's face, was also armed. Strapped to her leg was a knife holster, the knife, thankfully, still in situ. Although The Pan wondered how long for.

'Who are you?' she said.

'The Pan of Hamgee,' mumbled The Pan.

The stranger's arm shot out, grabbing The Pan's neck, pushing his head up. 'What?'

'I'm The Pan of Hamgee,' said The Pan, more clearly this time, although it was difficult when the woman had such a firm grip on his neck.

'What are you doing causing a ruckus on my patch?' she asked, squeezing The Pan's neck a bit tighter and stepping towards him in a way that made her biceps bulge intimidatingly under her shirt. Blimey she was ripped; and a poser, to boot. The Pan bet she'd practiced that move. Probably best not to mention that though.

'I don't want to cause any trouble.'

'But you have,' the other snarled, moving even closer to The Pan so their noses were touching. The Pan didn't even attempt eye contact, but fixed his gaze on a scar above the lady thug's left eye and kept it there.

'I'm very sorry.'

'Yeh, you will be.' She released her grip on The Pan,

pushing him back against the fellow behind who was pinning his arms. It was the muscly one he'd dodged earlier and it felt like being pushed against a rock.

The leader turned towards Killer Mike who was standing a few feet away. 'What are you doing chasing this little cretin across my real estate?'

'The thieving smeck robbed me!' said Killer Mike.

The pirate-like gang leader tutted. 'Nobody steals round here without my permission. This part of the city belongs to us, right boys?' The 'boys' in the gang dutifully agreed. 'So he's a thief you say,' the gang leader quizzed Killer Mike.

'Yer.'

'Let's see what he's stolen.'

'No wait! This isn't—' began The Pan and instead of drawing the knife, as he'd expected, the thug put one hand behind her and pulled a gun from her back pocket. It was an ancient pistol, a flintlock design, but at close range, that didn't make it any less deadly than a more modern piece of weaponry.

'Let me put that another way. Am I going to blow your brains out, or are you going to stand still and let us search you?' Smiling nastily, she put the muzzle of the gun to The Pan's forehead. Arnold, the Prophet! Please let the safety be on. The woman was clearly a psycho and more than likely to shoot by mistake. The Pan stood extremely still. 'Lads?'

She stepped back, gesturing at the rest of the gang. Much to The Pan's relief she put the gun back in her belt and moved even further out of the way to give her minions room. Clearly conducting the search herself was beneath her pay grade. Two of the gang rushed in and patted The Pan down. Naturally, they found the box at once, even in the secret poacher's pocket of his cloak. Arnold's trousers, that was all he needed. The thug took the box from her acolyte, opened it and whistled.

There was a pause as the gang members nearby,

members of Killer Mike's posse and a few locals who'd appeared from the buildings around them, craned to get a look at the sapphire and diamond earrings the box contained.

Arnold's conkers, no! Big Merv would throw a fit if The Pan lost these. The kind of fit that involved throwing The Pan in the river with concrete boots on. He had to get out of this spot somehow. 'That's not what I nicked from Killer—' began The Pan but the gang leader spoke across him.

'That is serious theft,' the woman told The Pan. 'I have some respect for you, stealing gear like that. But not when you take it from this guy.' She held out her hand and gestured to Killer Mike.

'No-no you don't understand. I didn't—'

'Does he look rich to you?'

'No, but those aren't—'

'Does he look like he can afford to buy something like these every day?'

'No, but I didn't steal them from him, I—'

'You bought them?' Everyone laughed.

This time The Pan did roll his eyes. 'Of course I smecking didn't! I'm worse off than he is!'

'Is that why you stole them from him?'

'NO, I didn't steal *those*! Not from—'

'Then who did? Mr Nobody?'

'No.' Everyone laughed again.

'So they're yours, are they?' asked the gang leader in a tone that said, 'yeh right' more eloquently than actually framing the phrase.

'Of course not, they're—'

'So you *did* steal them.'

'No,' said The Pan. 'If you'd just listen for one minute! I collected them.' Should he mention Big Merv here? No.

That would break every law of gangland protocol and just get The Pan into worse trouble.

'Who for?'

'Just ... someone.'

'Some bloke you met on the street.'

'No, my BOSS. He asked me to collect the earrings and deliver them.' The Pan congratulated himself on giving the word 'boss' capital letters, but the daft cow didn't pick up on it.

'Yeh, yeh, I'm sure. Because I bet you have a steady job.'

'Fair play, it's not steady. But it is a job and it's all I've got. If you don't believe me come back to the shop with me and we can ask the jeweller. He'll vouch for me.'

Silence. Was the gang boss thinking? The Pan suspected that, even if she was, this particular lady wasn't going to do something sensible like go back to the jewellers and get it all sorted out. Not when she could beat up The Pan for 'stealing' and then keep the earrings herself. The Pan had met enough beings like this one to know that the whole thing was just a ruse to get them off him. They were definitely a lot ritzier than the plain gold hoops she wore. It wasn't helping that the other moron still had The Pan's arms pinned behind his back. He did a lot of talking with his hands and every time he unconsciously tried to gesticulate, the idiot pulled his elbows even further together. His shoulders were aching and he had pins and needles in his fingers. Worse, not being able to wave his hands occasionally seemed to be hampering his ability to put his words in the right order, and he really needed to be articulate. He wanted to make it clear to the crowd what was happening. That way, in a few moments, when the lady thug invited the mob to give The Pan a good kicking, some of them might decide not to join in.

He watched her pretending to think. Trust his luck to get

a total smecker like this one. He might be petrified of Big Merv, but he knew that The Big Thing, though harsh, was usually fair. Yeh, Big Merv would have handled this a lot differently.

Finally, the thug spoke. 'People, do we have a wise guy on our hands?' She turned a circle, nodding at the crowd. 'I think we do have a wise guy.'

'No', The Pan said. 'Really. Not intentionally. Look if you'd just come back to the shop with me? They'll explain—'

The gang leader spoke over him. 'You know what we do to wise guys round here, right boys? Especially when they're thieves.'

'Yer, we punish them, right Marcella?' said a deep voice from behind The Pan, the one that had his arms pinned.

'That's right, Melton. We punish them,' said the gang leader, or Marcella, as The Pan now knew she was called.

Marvellous.

Killer Mike flashed The Pan a nasty smile and snickered.

'Go on then, tell us why you're innocent, you piece of crap. We're gagging to hear,' Marcella ordered him.

Again, silence fell.

'K— Mike runs a butcher's stall up in Upper Right. I asked if I could help him out in return for food. He said yes. I worked on his stall all morning and at the end he refused to pay me, threatened me and told me to get lost. So yes, I nicked a pie. It was wrong of me but I was hungry and I worked a lot longer, for nothing, than that pie was worth. But the pie is all I nicked. The earrings have nothing to do with this.'

'Ah poor ickle fellow,' said Marcella (Arnold! She was a total get) 'did the nasty bad man take advantage of you? I tell you what. I'll take these earrings and return them to their rightful owner.'

'Yeh right, I'm sure you will,' muttered The Pan, his

mouth running away without his brain as usual.

'What did you say?' Marcella got up close to him again, her nose inches from The Pan's.

Bum. Why couldn't he ever learn to shut up? The Pan had never been a fighter—his skill set was running—but he couldn't run unless the fellow pinning his arms let go. Arnold, even if he just shifted his grip for a moment, The Pan thought he might be able to wriggle free. But 'Melton' was clearly a pro. Worse, he was holding so tightly that The Pan's arms had now completely gone to sleep. Never mind, at least that meant they hurt less.

'Finicky B— I mean, Flynn and Flynn on Tarbot Street knows who the earrings are for,' said The Pan. He wished, heartily, that he'd had the presence of mind to double back to the jeweller's when he'd met Killer Mike, instead of just running willy nilly. He'd been an idiot. Too late now.

'You're lying,' said Marcella.

'I'm not,' retorted The Pan. Nooo, don't contradict a nutter like this directly. He started again. 'Look, I don't want any trouble and I'm sorry to have inconvenienced you by being chased across your patch but if you'd just let me go, I promise I'll never, ever—'

'Yeh, yeh.'

There was a crack and blinding pain as Marcella head-butted him. He felt himself falling as Melton finally let go of his arms. The Pan tried to persuade them to move but they were nothing but numb lumps of meat and were having none of it. Then the ground came up to meet him and he turned his head sideways to try to lessen the impact as his face hit the cobbles. Never mind, it could have been worse—from what he could feel, his nose was still in one piece, although he thought it was probably bleeding. And as far as he could tell his teeth were still all there.

Marcella put her foot on The Pan's head and waited,

giving the crowd time to laugh and jeer, and for their appetite for a spectacle to grow. Arnold's conkers, it looked as if this was it. The Pan had always assumed it would be the Grongles who killed him, not his own kind. Yet despite the direness of his situation, something in him refused to believe that this was the end of the road. Still he searched for a way to resolve the situation and get out alive, the way he always did.

Ignoring the mocking faces, The Pan desperately scanned the sea of legs in his field of vision, looking hopelessly for anything that might help. That's when he saw it, half hidden, right at the back—a movement as someone squatted down to try and catch his eye. Someone who wasn't joining in; someone he knew. Fred 'Fingers' Davies; one of the slickest pickpockets in Ning Dang Po and a fellow punter at The Parrot and Screwdriver. That was a surprise. Fred swore that a crowd was the best place to work but The Pan had assumed the crowds in question would be more well-heeled than this one. As his eyes met The Pan's, Fred raised his hand and put one finger against the side of his nose.

It was bad form to ask for aid, especially in a situation where it would be impossible to give. But even so, before he could stop himself, The Pan's mouth formed the silent plea, 'Help me!'

He swore he saw Fred wink and hold up his hand, first finger and thumb joined together in the universal sign language for the word 'OK'. Then The Pan's attention was rapidly focused back on Marcella.

'Let's show this little smecker what we do to thieving scumbags, boys!' she shouted and removed her foot from The Pan's head, but unfortunately, only to take a good swing with her leg. All sight of Fred was lost as The Pan rolled to dodge the hefty kick Marcella aimed into his face.

Unfortunately, the impact of it still hit him but in the stomach, knocking the wind out of him. He lay on his back, wheezing, as his assailant squatted down beside him holding the box The Pan was supposed to deliver in front of his face.

'I'll take this,' she laughed nastily as The Pan rolled around trying to catch his breath with a highly embarrassing barking noise. 'And in return, you get to live. But if I ever see you around here again, I'll kill you.'

Stuff gangland protocol, The Pan thought, and decided to explain that the box was Big Merv's. But he was still winded and all that came out was an asthmatic hiss. Oh well, even if he'd been able to speak, it probably wouldn't have made any difference.

Marcella stood up and faced Killer Mike, putting the earrings in her jacket pocket. The crowd of onlookers pressed in, clearly hoping things were about to kick off. Marcella didn't disappoint them. 'Alright boys, I've promised I won't kill him. But we're still going to teach this little cleggnut a lesson, aren't we?'

'Yeeeeeh!' they screamed.

The Pan rolled and tried to escape the well-rehearsed efforts of Marcella's gang without much success. It didn't hurt as much as he expected—perhaps they were knackered from kicking the living daylights out of whoever it was they'd been beating up on the stairs. No. That wasn't it. It was because Killer Mike and his mates had joined in, not to mention some of the onlookers. While enthusiastic, none of them were experts by any means. They crowded in close while Marcella's slightly more disciplined bruisers tried to hold them back. The Pan started crawling towards the passageway out of the courtyard. The baying crowd followed, closing in, jostling and pushing to get a kick at him. And then one of the bystanders kicked one of Marcella's goons by mistake, and the goon lost his balance and fell over. He was kicked, in turn, by one of the likely lads who'd joined in the chase with Killer Mike. Then there was shouting and one of Marcella's other goons punched Killer Mike's goon and in a moment, the two parties were fighting each other, their quarry forgotten.

The Pan, bruised and bleeding, crawled quickly through the forest of swinging, bovver-booted legs to the passage that led back to the market, and freedom. He momentarily wondered if he should wait for Fred. But there was no sign of him and The Pan knew that if he wanted to escape it was time to get moving.

'Stop, you morons!' shouted Marcella. 'He's getting away.'

But it was too late. Both gangs were far too busy fighting and her commands fell on deaf ears. The Pan's ankle was hurting and he didn't dare climb so he limped out onto Tarbot Street as fast as he could. They'd be after him soon enough but he was pretty sure they'd assume he'd taken the quickest route out, which would be back the way he'd come, via the canal.

Right, so which way should he *actually* go then? He wondered if he should go back to the jeweller's shop and explain what happened. Finicky Bert had seemed kind and— No. Not if this lot followed him. The Pan didn't want to bring that kind of trouble to the old boy's door.

Best go in the opposite direction to the one they'd expect then. He took off his hat and cloak, holding them in front of him so that from behind he was just a tousle-haired bloke in a coat. Then, he took a deep breath, and did one of the bravest things he'd ever done. He limped up to the junction at the other end of the street and turned onto Outgate: a route which would lead him through the very heart of Marcella's territory and into a lot more trouble, if his pursuers realised and caught up with him.

Holding his side, which ached where Marcella had kicked him, and with his distinctive hat and cloak still bundled up but now tucked under one arm, The Pan moved as fast as he could through the centre of Marcella's patch and out the other side, towards the safety of Pollock Street at the far end. Once he was sure he was entirely off Marcella's ground and that he wasn't being followed, he stopped to get his breath back, and put his cloak and hat back on again.

Upside to the situation? He was alive. Downside? He'd lost the item he was supposed to be delivering. So the whole 'alive' thing might prove to be temporary.

What now?

He didn't know.

His nose was bleeding and he could feel another warm trickle of blood running down the side of his face. What to do?

He started to walk. Dazed and miserable, he wandered the streets racking his brains to think of a solution. But none came. He could sell his wheels—wait, no, he couldn't sell his wheels because he needed somewhere to sleep. He wouldn't always be able to find an empty greenhouse or garden shed. Anyway, since his snurd wouldn't begin to cover the cost of those earrings, there was no point. Furthermore, by the time Gerry had finished working on it, there'd be no time to get a decent price before the evening *and* buy replacement jewellery for Big Merv's friend, Ms Myrtle.

Maybe he could go back to the jewellers and—

No.

The Pan walked on. Dusk came, darkness fell and still he blundered through the streets. After some time, he realised he'd found his way onto Dumpty Street. He followed it to its end, where it came out onto Market Square. Turnadot Street was just over the other side, a few hundred yards from where he stood. He thought longingly of the Parrot and Screwdriver. No, he couldn't go into the pub in this state. He blundered across the road, through the traffic, to the park in the middle. He sat on a bench and put his head in his hands.

This was it. The end of the line. He checked his watch but it was gone, torn off or broken during the melee earlier, presumably. 'Bastards,' said The Pan miserably.

He looked up at the clock on the front of Mrs Ormaloo's laundry and darning service on the corner of Dumpty Street. It said six. In two hours, at eight pm, The Pan would have to head over to the address in The Planes anyway, so he could explain to Ms Myrtle what had happened to the present Big Merv had bought her. That would be fun, but probably marginally less grim than the conversation he was likely to be having with Big Merv shortly afterwards.

Chapter 6
Despair and deliverance

Sitting miserably in the park in Market Square The Pan looked up at the sky. There was no point in giving up like this. He had to think. He'd got out of worse scrapes before. Actually, when he thought about it, no he hadn't, or at least, not unless he counted his whole life since being blacklisted. Surely, there had to be a way. 'Right then, let's work this out,' he told himself.

First of all, the facts. The jewellery he was supposed to deliver had gone. All he had was a card which Big Merv had given him with the instructions. He was supposed to have put it inside the box when he'd collected it. '"Happy birthday sweets",' The Pan read aloud. 'Smeckity-smeck! Where am I going to get a pair of diamond and sapphire earrings by this evening?'

He looked at his watch and was once again confronted with an empty wrist. But a check on the clock on the front of Mrs Ormaloo's revealed that only a couple of minutes had passed since he last looked. 'Two hours,' he told himself. 'You have two hours to sort this out or you will become one with the outer ring.'

Or it would be a swim in the river with concrete boots on.

Arnold! No. Not that. The thought of drowning, be it in the river or in the rapidly hardening concrete of a newly constructed motorway stanchion, filled The Pan with dread. Just the idea made him start shaking uncontrollably. He hiccupped and leaned forward. Was he going to hurl? No. He hadn't eaten anything since breakfast for starters. He was just shocked from this afternoon, that was all.

No. The Pan knew this wasn't shock. It was rank fear. He put his head in his hands again. He felt like crying. Not that it would do any good.

He was so wrapped up in his misery that he didn't hear the sound of footsteps as somebody approached. He didn't even register when the person came and stood in front of him, until the newcomer spoke. 'Is you alright, mate?'

'Trev?' The Pan looked up at the sizeable form of the son of Gladys from the Parrot and Screwdriver.

'Arnold, lad!' said Trev, immediately squatting down so his head was level with The Pan's. 'What's happened to you? You is proper smashed up.'

Trev's kindly expression and the sympathy in his voice made The Pan feel even more wobbly. 'Yeh. It's been a rough day.'

'C'mon, I reckons you is not goin' ter help yer self stayin' here. You has ter come home with me. Mum an' Aunt Ada will fix you up.' With that, Trev hooked his arm under The Pan's and helped him to his feet. 'Easy. Take a few deep breaths, son.'

The Pan nodded. His legs were really wobbly now. Too much adrenaline and too long a walk, he supposed. Arnold's snot, he had to walk up to The Planes later.

'Ready?'

'Yeh. It's alright Trev, I can walk on my own.'

'You reckons?'

'Yeh.'

'Alright, but if you needs help, mind, you tell me.'

'Will do. Thanks.'

Slowly, they started across the park towards the crossing nearest the end of Turnadot Street. The thought of The Parrot and Screwdriver somehow put new heart into The Pan. 'It's not as bad as it looks I expect,' he said. 'I'm stiff more than anything.'

'Whatever you says, lad. By The Prophet, what in Arnold's name has you been doing?'

'I got chased.'

'I reckons you got caught proper too.'

'Yeh.' The Pan chuckled, which hurt a bit. 'Ouch. You're not wrong there.'

'Who done this to you?'

'Someone called Marcella.'

'Not Marcella the Pirate?' asked Trev as The Pan walked stiffly beside him down Turnadot Street.

'I dunno, but if it helps, she wears a bandana and plaits her hair so she looks like an octopus on a stalk. She pulled a gun on me,' said The Pan.

Trev out-and-out laughed and then, noticing afresh the state The Pan was in, looked guilty. 'That's Marcella the Pirate alright. Where's she hanging out these days, then?'

'Tarbot Quay,' mumbled The Pan.

'That's bad luck, lad. Last I heard she was moving to Glardy.'

'Pity she didn't,' said The Pan, with feeling.

'Right.' Trev sucked air in through his teeth. 'You got yerself into a spot of bother?' he asked, as they neared The Parrot and Screwdriver pub.

'A bit.'

'Looks like more an' a bit, son,' said Trev. 'Let's go in round the back way,' he added, steering The Pan into the alley between the pub and its coach house opposite. 'Does you need a bit of help getting yerself out of trouble?'

'I don't think anyone can sort it.'

'Mum reckons there isn't nothing that can't be sorted if you thinks about it hard enough.'

'She's right up to a point. In fact, usually, I'd agree with her, but I think even *she* might be stymied by this one.'

Trev held the back door open. Just the smell of the

Parrot and Screwdriver's back hall, of baking bread and biscuits with a dash of beery yeastiness, made The Pan feel calmer and more hopeful. Surely Big Merv would be reasonable about this. Surely he wouldn't blame The Pan for being rolled over by some small-time gangster. Big Merv owned Ning Dang Po so Marcella probably worked for him anyway. Yes, so if Big Merv's staff stepped out of line it wasn't The Pan's fault and the earrings would come to light soon enough. Maybe if he explained what happened ... Or perhaps if he went to see Bob—she was a kindly maternal type. Maybe she would be able to soften the blow, give Big Merv the bad news before The Pan had to. Or maybe Ms Myrtle would help. She was the intended recipient of the earrings and she'd seemed sympathetic when The Pan met her before. 'I think I'm just going to have to go and explain myself and hope I'm forgiven.'

Trev gave him a bit of a look as if to say 'that's really going to work,' but he was tactful enough not to voice his opinion. Instead he said, 'If that's what you is going ter do then you can't go up there looking like you does. Get yerself upstairs to the flat an' Mum and Aunt Ada'll be up in a sec to get you sorted.'

'Aren't they serving? Shouldn't I wait until they—'

'Ner. 'S no bother. 'S quiet tonight an' I can take care of the bar. Best go in the kitchen. Second door on the right. Is you goin' ter be alright on the stairs?'

'Yeh. I'll be fine. And thank you,' said The Pan.

Trev gave The Pan's shoulder an avuncular pat. 'On you go son. Mum and Aunt Ada'll be up in a two ticks.'

****

Gladys and Ada's kitchen was small and snug, with cream cupboards and a stainless steel sink. There was a cooker, an old-fashioned looking fridge and a compact chest-style freezer. On top of the cupboards were bottles of home-made chutney and, unfortunately, Humbert, the pub's resident parrot.

'Futtocks!' he shouted as The Pan walked in.

'Hello Humbert.'

The Pan took a seat at the kitchen table, which was oblong with round corners and had a Formica top decorated with a speckled pattern in shades of red and black. Humbert flapped down from the cupboard top and sat on his shoulder. It didn't hurt as much as he expected.

'Polly want a cracker?' said Humbert. Unusually, he appeared to be asking a question rather than making demands.

'Not right now, thanks,' said The Pan.

'Rope my futtocks?' Humbert sidled towards his head and nibbled his ear gently.

'Thanks, but no.'

The sound of Gladys and Ada approaching could be heard from the hall.

'Humbert! Get off that poor boy!' said Ada as she swept into the room. In one hand she held a pair of scissors, and in the other, a large plastic box with a red cross on it.

'Polish my melons!' shouted Humbert.

'Out! This minute! Go on! This is no place for a parrot.'

'Yer, it's s'posed ter be sterile.'

'Wipe my conkers?'

'No, Humbert.'

Ada's infernal pet hopped off The Pan's shoulder, did a quick circuit round the room and flew out into the hall.

'Trev'll look after him,' said Ada as the parrot headed down the stairs. The Pan found himself feeling a little sorry for Trev. She closed the door to stop Humbert from coming back in.

'I reckons you needs a resto— restorative,' said Gladys dumping a brandy balloon on the table in front of him. ''S calvados. Good for shock.'

But probably not for concussion. Never mind. The Pan wasn't one hundred percent certain he'd been concussed so he took it gratefully and tossed half of it back in a gulp. The disapproval emanating from the old ladies was so strong it was almost like a solid entity, but he was too busy trying to breathe to apologise. 'Blimey!' he croaked.

'Yer. You isn't meant ter knock it back like some drunkard! 'S for sipping that is.'

'Yes, sorry,' wheezed The Pan. 'I'll remember next time.'

'Yer, you do that,' said Gladys sternly, but there was a twinkle in the corner of her eye. 'Now hold still.'

The Pan sat at the table and let the old ladies fuss round him with a bowl of water, disinfectant, plasters and antiseptic cream. As the warm glow of the calvados spread from his stomach Gladys and Ada gently washed the blood from his face with cotton wool. They examined the damage and Gladys sucked the air in through her teeth several times, the same way Gerry did when he was evaluating some problem with The Pan's wheels.

'I have absolutely no idea how you come out of these things with all your teeth, young man,' said Ada as the two old ladies clucked and tutted round him.

"S right. Most fellas who does what you does needs dentures by this time. You hasn't had yer nose broken neither. 'S a miracle I reckons,' agreed Gladys.

'Yes, it's all minor cuts and bruises. Fred "Fingers" Davies is in tonight and if what he says is to be believed, you are very lucky.'

'Yer,' said Gladys as she dabbed cream on The Pan's face.

'It's alright, I can do that myself, you know,' he said.

'Yer, you can but I knows you. You'll make a pig's breakfast of it.'

'Exactly,' Ada agreed. 'Much better we do it. You don't want to go around looking as if you're wearing clown makeup.'

'Yer, 's got ter be subtle hasn't it?' sad Gladys.

'Well, yes, I would prefer it that way,' replied The Pan

'Yer, I s'pects you would. An' that's why you isn't doin' it.'

'Exactly,' agreed Ada. 'You'd put the whole tube on at once and end up looking like a bad variety act. There now,' she added. 'All done. We have to go back to the bar, but Fred's down there looking for you. He seems to be in a bit of a state—'

'Yer, says it is private business,' said Gladys, making a face as she rammed the plasters, scissors and other medical accoutrements back into the first aid box.

'That's right, dear. Would you like to use the snug?'

'Yer, we can keep it quiet if you likes.'

'Thanks,' said The Pan getting stiffly to his feet. 'I'll just go down there, shall I?'

'Yer, we'll send Fred through,' said Gladys.

'Yes, dear,' added Ada.

Picking up the brandy balloon which was still half full of Gladys' homemade calvados, The Pan headed downstairs. He wondered what Fred wanted to say. Sorry probably. But there was nothing to forgive. After all, it wasn't as if he could have helped The Pan—he'd have just got beaten up himself.

****

The snug was a small wooden-panelled room lined with ancient books and furnished with a low table, two comfy chairs and a sofa. A warm fire burned brightly in the grate. It was homely and The Pan wished he could just lie on the sofa and go to sleep. However Fred was already in position, waiting for him in one of the comfy chairs. The Pan took the other one at the opposite end of the long, low table. 'Hi Fred,' he said, raising his glass. 'Cheers.' He spoke with a relaxed calm he didn't remotely feel.

Fred raised his pint schooner, gulped back half the contents and got straight down to business. 'I've been looking all over for you, son,' he said.

'You have?'

'Course. See, sonny, you and I, we've got to have a chat.'

'Does it have to be now? I'll have a lot more time later. If I'm still alive, that is.'

'Yeh, the still-alive thing—that's why it has to be now, laddie.'

'OK.'

'What you going to do about this morning's little caper?'

'What can I do?'

'Weeell, you're Big Merv's delivery man and you were rolled over by a rival gang. That's where I'd start, although only if I didn't know what I'm about to tell you now.'

'Which is?'

'That jeweller's a shyster. The earrings were all paste and cheap metal. They was blummin' good, mind, but they were fake as fake. I dunno what Big Merv paid for those but I can tell you for nothing, he was robbed.'

'Mmm. I know how that feels.'

'Yeh,' Fred was quiet for a moment. 'That didn't look much fun today, lad.'

'It wasn't.' The two of them sat in silence for a moment.

'I'm sorry I couldn't help you out, sonny.'

Fred was the slipperiest crook out there, but the look of angst on his face seemed pretty genuine to The Pan. Either that or he was one of the best actors in K'Barthan history. Maybe a bit of both. 'It's OK. After all, you were outnumbered a bit, unless you're a ninja. Are you a ninja, Fred?' The Pan asked, trying to make light of it. He grinned, but it hurt his face and he suspected it came out as more of a grimace.

'If I am a ninja, it's only at picking pockets.' Fred put his hand in the breast pocket of his jacket and pulled out a leather box. It was dark blue, with a line of gold leaf around the edge. By the Prophet's bum! Was that what The Pan thought it was?

Fred handed it to him. 'It isn't what you think.'

'It isn't?' asked The Pan trying to hide his disappointment. No, of course it wasn't, it was in a bigger box.

'Nope,' said Fred, confirming his fears. 'It's better.'

The Pan opened the box. 'Smecking Arnold!' he said before he could stop himself. Inside was a sapphire and diamond necklace. Delicate, intricate and clearly top quality. It was obvious that it had been made by the same jeweller who'd made the earrings as it followed the same design cues. Indeed, it almost looked as if it was made to go with the earrings but, in The Pan's view, it was somehow more delicate—prettier.

'I've been wondering what I could do with that for a long time,' said Fred.

'I can't take this. In fact, to be honest, you shouldn't have either.'

'It's not like it looks, lad. See, I know what goes on round that jewellers, cause sometimes people who've just bought jewellery tend to be excited, and happy and you know ...' he shrugged.

'Not very careful with it?'

'Exactly. Things get lost don't they?'

'Mmm, I'm sure they do.' Yeh, especially when Fred was around.

'That's right, lad. I'm just teaching folks to look after their stuff. Some Grongle fellah lost this a couple of months back. I've been waiting for the right time to sell it but truth is, some stuff is too good and too conspicuous to sell.'

Was this the truth or just a story to mollify any shred of

principles The Pan might have? 'It's fantastic of you Fred, but I can't take it. For a start, it's your living and—'

'I'm making plenty of living, thanks. Not to mention the fact that it's easy enough to spare something I can't sell. I could break it up but I'd not realise half its value, so I may as well put it to good use. "*The Prophet looks well on charity*", son: Sayings of The Prophet, Book Two, Chapter Three, Verse One.' Fred winked.

'I still can't take it, Fred. I mean, what's Big Merv going to say when he finds out I've delivered the wrong thing?'

'Ah, Big Merv. Well lad, it isn't what Big Merv thinks that you have to worry about—it's what the lady thinks. If she likes it, he'll be happy enough. And trust me, you don't want to give her those earrings.'

'Have you got them?'

'Not as such.'

'Seriously Fred, if you have any way of getting those earrings then yes, I do want to give them to her.'

'No, you don't. I told you! They're fake.'

Were they though? Or was this just Fred being ... Fred? 'It doesn't matter. I'm only the messenger. I don't need to think. I just do what I'm told.'

'Ah, they all say that. But you're different—you *do* need to think.' Fred put one finger against his temple and tapped it. 'What if I could get you the earrings and you delivered them then Big Merv found out they were fake. You think that jeweller's going to 'fess up?'

He'd seemed like a lovely old boy but— 'Thinking about it, no.'

'See, now you're cooking. What would you do in his position?'

'Run away.'

'Or?'

'OK, you're right, I'd probably find someone to blame. Or

at least some reason for it not to be my fault.'

'You're a bit kinder than most though, aren't you? That's your problem right there. You're stuck with the life you lead and no-one can fix that, but you care too much to be a natural crook. Thing is, if that jeweller's bent, it means he had a choice. That means he isn't going to care like you do. And I know, and I reckon you know, that what *he'll* do is put the finger on you. And then my son, you *will* be in a sticky situation.'

'The situation's looking pretty sticky as it is, Fred.'

'Nah. All you have to do is deliver the box and keep schtum.'

'Big Merv's going to notice.'

'Yes, but the big picture here is that he wants the lady to get a nice prezzie and it don't get much nicer than that!' Fred jabbed a finger at the box on the table. 'Technically, all you've done is pick up a box from the jeweller's and deliver it. There's no reason for you to know that what's in there isn't what was officially in there originally, even if you do know unofficially.'

The Pan frowned. 'Can you put that any more clearly, Fred?'

'We're pretending the whole sorry episode with Marcella the Pirate never happened. You picked up a box from the jewellers and delivered it without opening it to see what was in it.'

'Yeh, well, I'm supposed to put a card in. Here,' The Pan took the card out of his jacket pocket and showed it to Fred.

'Pity about the bloodstain. But I doubt anyone'll notice. So, you put the card in. You're in the clear coz you still don't know it was earrings you was collecting. You picked up a box and you delivered one. If the fellow in the jeweller's gave you the wrong stuff that's his lookout. Big Merv wanted to give the lady some bling. You've got some bling, made by the same bloke, in a box that looks similar.'

The Pan stood up and began to pace the room. No. Don't get excited and just belt off to deliver it—think for a moment first. He stopped and sat down again.

'There you go. Home free lad,' said Fred. 'It looks near enough and she gets some jewellery like Big Merv wants. It's true that a few loose ends aren't going to tie up but trust me, it's close enough.'

The Pan sat and stared at the box. On one level, this had to be the stupidest idea imaginable. On another, it might just work. And Arnold The Prophet knew it was better than doing nothing and becoming one with the outer ring ... well ... just and— hang on. 'Fred, seriously, have you got the original earrings?'

'Why?'

'I was just thinking that if you had, and there was some way to get them back into the shop, you know, so the jeweller really has muddled them up?'

Fred's face lit up with a mischievous smile. 'Now that's using your brain, son. It'll do that jeweller's head in! He deserves it, cocky sod! Ripping off The Big Thing,' he stood up and shook The Pan's hand. 'I'd better be off. I'm not saying I have those earrings, mind, but I know where they are so it's the same thing. I can get hold of them easily enough.' He winked again and The Pan reflected that it wasn't just the jeweller who was cocky. Then again, Fred had good reason—The Pan had every confidence that wherever the earrings were now, they'd be in Fred's pocket in an hour or two. 'I'll see what I can do. Don't you worry, laddo. You just take that box up to The Planes and hand it over.'

'Thanks Fred.'

'Any time, son. Right well, it's getting on, I'd better be off.'

'It is? What time is it?'

'Ah!' Fred held up one finger. 'That reminds me, before I go.' He took something from his inside pocket. 'This yours?'

The Pan's eyes widened at the sight of his watch. 'How did you—?'

'Nice piece,' said Fred conversationally.

'Arnold's armpits, Fred! You're a wonder. Thanks.'

Fred beamed. 'She's a nasty little squirt, that Marcella the Pirate,' he said as he handed the watch over. 'You want to remember that and steer well clear of her.'

'Thanks,' said The Pan as he strapped the watch back on to his wrist. 'Hang on! It's nearly eight o'clock!' he squeaked as he saw the time it read. 'Arnold's trollies, I'm supposed to be in The Planes about now!'

'Then you'd better fly, son!'

Chapter 7
Delivery

'I do believe you're late,' said Ms Myrtle, her tones as honeyed as ever. 'Big Merv told me to expect a delivery at eight. Unless you have a different delivery?'

'Yes. Sorry. I'm here with the eight o'clock delivery but you're right, I am late. I ran into a spot of bother on the way.'

'Come in.' She stood back and opened the door. 'Oh,' she said as The Pan stepped into the hall and she caught sight of his face. 'You did run into trouble, didn't you?'

'Nothing I couldn't handle,' lied The Pan.

Ms Myrtle's indulgent smile said, more eloquently than any words could, how unconvinced she was by his bravado. Then again, she had the good grace and tact not to point it out. 'So, what do you have for me?' she asked, sashaying through a doorway to the left. They walked into the same front reception room The Pan had been into on his previous visit when he'd dropped off a birthday present for Ms Myrtle's daughter.

'This,' said The Pan. He took off his hat, bowed low and then produced the box from his coat pocket with what would have been a flourish if it hadn't got caught in the lining and ruined the effect somewhat.

'Thank you.' She opened the box and gasped. The Pan hoped, with all his heart, that it was the right kind of gasp. No. Of course it was—her eyes shone as she read the card. Fred was wrong about the blood though. She noticed, because she looked sharply at The Pan with an expression of concern. 'Is the thumbprint yours?'

'Yes. Sorry. If it helps, it is my blood and not someone else's.'

She smiled kindly and The Pan's heart melted a little. She was very lovely, was Ms Myrtle.

'From the "spot of bother"?'

'Yes, I—'

Footsteps strode down the hall and Big Merv's sizeable bulk filled the doorway. 'C'mon sweets, we gotta go.' Ms Myrtle turned to him with a smile that could have turned the hardest heart to butter but which appeared to have no effect on Big Merv, mainly because he was too busy glaring at The Pan. 'You're late, you snotty little Herbert.'

'Yeh. I'm sorry,' said The Pan.

'Darling,' cooed Ms Myrtle, finally getting Big Merv's attention, 'your delivery has just arrived.'

'Yer, late.'

'Oh but better late than never, my love! It's so beautiful.' She sashayed across the room, wrapped her arms around his neck and gave him a long, lingering kiss on the cheek.

Blimey. The Pan looked down at his feet.

'Can you put it on for me?' She held the box out to Big Merv.

Big Merv's voice was a little softer when he said 'Sure treacle.' He took the box from her and she turned with her back to him.

The Pan noticed his expression of surprise and watched as unbeknown to Ms Myrtle, Big Merv looked at the box and frowned. Arnold's sweaty armpits! He'd clearly noticed the bloody thumbprint on the card as well. His green eyes narrowed as he took out the necklace and put the box on a nearby shelf. He put it gently round her neck and fastened it at the back. All the while he kept his gaze on The Pan, his face hard, his eyes glittering with ... no, it wasn't anger. His antennae were waving to and fro. Thought? Yeh, The Pan could almost see the mental cogs working.

This was the time to look innocent, he remembered. He

had to be completely ignorant of the fact that the necklace wasn't the jewellery Big Merv had ordered. Except The Pan wasn't much good at innocent: so he went for a perplexed vibe instead; a kind of what-have-I-done face. He doubted it had worked.

It was only a few seconds of eye contact, but Big Merv was the boss because he was smart. The Pan knew he could read other beings; know what they were actually thinking rather than what they wanted him to believe. Time seemed to stand still, and The Pan had a horrible feeling his boss had seen straight through his act. Then Big Merv looked down and concentrated on the extra safety chain which had a fiddlier catch than the main one.

'There you go, babe,' he said. Ms Myrtle turned to face him and again his expression softened. 'C'mon sweets, let's go.'

With a gentle hand on her back he ushered her towards the hall. She went ahead of him but in the doorway, Big Merv turned. 'I wanna know why you were late, you little scrote,' he told The Pan. 'I want you waiting for me at the Big Thing at ten o'clock tomorrow morning with a smecking good explanation. You get me?'

'Yes, Boss.'

'Good. An' make sure you be there. Don't make me come looking for you.'

'No, Boss.'

'Now get out.'

Big Merv strode down the hall and opened the door. With an apologetic look at Ms Myrtle, The Pan followed after him and stepped through the door, which The Big Thing was holding open, into the night. The security gates were open and Big Merv's shiny midnight blue MKII snurd was waiting at the bottom of the stairs. Bob the Blaggysomp was standing by the back door with a dark uniform and peaked cap on, ready to open it for Ms Myrtle. She nodded a hello as The Pan passed her.

'Hi Bob.' The Pan walked away into the darkness without looking back.

Chapter 8
Debrief

The Pan waited at The Big Thing nightclub the next morning in a state of some agitation.

On the plus side, he'd delivered a box that looked, in every way, like the box he was supposed to deliver to Ms Myrtle on Big Merv's behalf. On the downside Big Merv looked properly annoyed that it wasn't the original. And The Pan's efforts to feign innocence clearly hadn't worked. Unless Big Merv's anger was down to the fact his messenger had arrived a few minutes late ...? Was it that? Well, it was more like half an hour, so it could have been. Yes. Oh please, please yes, Arnold let it be that.

Big Merv kept The Pan waiting, so he sat on a chair in the hall, flanked by two of the larger enforcers Big Merv employed. As time passed he got more and more nervous.

At last, an elderly Galorsh came out of Big Merv's office. He was wearing a smart suit and his furry purple tail was folded neatly round and dangled over one arm. With a cheery goodbye to Big Merv, he closed the door and started across the reception area to the stairs. As he passed, The Pan recognised him as the recipient of an earlier delivery—his name was Arnhelm Gaspot. Mr Gaspot also recognised The Pan and stopped. 'Hello there, young fellow,' he said.

'Hi Mr Gaspot,' said The Pan, scrambling as hurriedly to his feet as his recent injuries would allow and shaking the old fellow's hand.

'My, my! You have been in the wars.'

'Just a spot of bother,' The Pan smiled. 'Occupational hazard.'

'I see. This is Big Merv's most reliable delivery man,' Mr Gaspot told the two silent heavies standing either side of The Pan. 'I hope it wasn't another run in with those oiks who were after you when you brought us our Arnold's Birthday pastries.'

'No, no.'

'Good. We sent them the wrong way, of course.'

'Most kind of you. It was a great help,' said The Pan, remembering his flight from the Grongles at the hotel where he'd delivered the pastries, and the Blurpons who'd helped him.

The door of Big Merv's office was flung open again. 'What are you doing, you little bleeder? Mr Gaspot ain't got time to stand around nattering to you,' said Big Merv tetchily. 'Inside. Pronto.'

The Pan forbore to mention that it was actually Mr Gaspot who'd stopped to talk to him. Instead, he waved the elderly creature an apologetic goodbye and followed Big Merv into his study. Inside, Frank was standing silently in the corner in his leather trench coat. It creaked as he folded his arms and looked daggers at The Pan. Not good. Neither Frank nor Harry liked The Pan, but of the two, Frank was the one whose dislike was the deepest. Not that there was much in it.

'Sit.' Big Merv pointed to a metal-framed stacking chair which had been placed in front of the desk. The Pan did as he was told. 'Ms Myrtle reckons you was late cause you had some trouble.'

'A little.'

Big Merv held up the card he'd given The Pan to put in the jewellery box. 'That your blood on there?'

'I'm afraid so.'

Big Merv's piercing felt-tip green eyes met The Pan's. 'Yer. I ain't surprised. Alright. What you done and what was the bother? And don't lie to me, pal, coz I ain't stupid.'

'I delivered a box to the address at The Planes, like you asked.'

'Harrumph,' said Frank.

'Alright, keep it down, Frank.'

'Sorry Boss.'

'You delivered *the* box or *a* box?'

Arnold's toe jam! The Pan knew exactly what to say here, and it was that he'd delivered the box Finicky Bert gave him. OK, so it was technically slander, but he didn't believe Bert would get into trouble. He was certainly old enough to have experienced a 'senior moment' and handed over the wrong box. However, faced with an angry Big Merv, The Pan found he couldn't bring himself to lie. 'I delivered *a* box,' mumbled The Pan.

'*A* box. Yer. See, my beef, son, is that the box you delivered ain't the box what you picked up.'

Arse. Rumbled. Now what? Think, man, think! The Pan sat without speaking for a moment as he racked his brains to come up with an explanation. He tried to sit quietly and not fidget, but the butterflies in his stomach made it difficult for him to stay still. He rubbed his sweaty hands together. Smeck! Any way he answered this, he was toast. Maybe he should just make a bolt for the door? No, Frank was quicker than he looked, and there were the big blokes in the hall. The Pan knew he'd just get thumped, tied up and put back where he was, only with even slimmer odds of survival than he had now. 'Ah.'

'Yer, "ah". So what I wanna know is,' Big Merv's felt-tip green eyes glared into The Pan's, 'what happened to the box, pal? The one with the earrings in.'

The Pan wanted to meet Big Merv's angry glare with a look of brave indifference, but instead his eyes slid downwards to his hands. He wiped his sweaty palms on his trousers. 'Look, to be honest, I think there was a bit of a mix up.' His voice sounded a lot squeakier than he wanted it to, and the way he was shaking had given it a kind of vibrato which didn't help his efforts to sound confident and manly. 'It might still be at the jewellers.'

'Yer, 's right, it is. I've had a word with Finicky Bert and all, but he don't know how it got there. Mr Gaspot there, what you've just met, he does my accounts, but he's also got a hobby. He's an expert on gems and such. He's had a look at that necklace and he says it's the real deal, which is what Finicky Bert said and all. A lot more real than the deal I got Ms Myrtle, if you get me.'

'The— the earrings were fake?'

'Yeh.' The Pan thought he could feel a blush rising, but it might have just been some kind of preparation-for-flight reflex. He wasn't sure. He could feel the hairs standing up on the back of his neck and cold sweat starting around his temples. He ran one hand through his hair. 'Well, I did run into some trouble. I picked up the box and that was fine but I didn't think I should wander round with it all day. I was going to go back to the Parrot and Screwdriver to ask Ada and Gladys to put it behind the bar for me. I thought, that way it'd be safe until it was time to deliver it. I'm not sure what happened, but I bumped into ... someone I shouldn't have.'

'Grongles? Or some bloke you nicked stuff off of?'

The Pan swallowed. 'Someone— the second one.'

'Who?'

'He's a butcher, runs a meat stall out in Upper Right, a bloke called Killer Mike,' gabbled The Pan. Why did his nervousness make him speak so fast? He stopped, took a breath and tried to ignore the way his heart was hammering. Frank leered at him nastily but Big Merv said nothing, letting The Pan fill the silence in his fear. 'The other day, I offered to help him out in return for a pie, but when I'd done a morning flogging his other pies, he said he'd changed his mind and refused to give me any payment. I'd worked hard and I didn't think a pie was much to ask in return. So I nicked one,' he said as he looked Big Merv in the eye for a few fleeting moments in an effort to accentuate the honesty of his answer.

'Yeh, yeh, spare us the sob story,' said Big Merv. Frank snorted. 'So you was unlucky.'

'Yes.'

'How big was that pie?'

The Pan held his hands out and drew a shape in the air about three inches by two. 'About so big.'

'An' that's all you done?'

'Yeh, unless someone else has stolen stuff from him and he thinks it's me. I try to rotate the stalls I ...' what was the right word? '... frequent. I only go to each stall every two or three months. I usually try to persuade them to give me food but some of them won't let me, you know, in case I'm—'

'A GBI?'

'Maybe.'

'Yer well, can't say as I blame 'em. You look the part, mate. I'd have had my doubts an' all if you hadn't been around so long.'

Little do you know, thought The Pan, but managed to stay silent.

'Alright, I wanna get this straight,' Big Merv continued, leaning back in his chair. It creaked ominously under the load. 'You nicked some of this geezer's wares and he is proper ticked off. Then you had the bad luck to run into 'im just after you collected the box I want delivered. Then what?'

'He shouted, "Stop thief!" and I ran away.'

'And ...?'

Hmm, how to answer this one? The Pan decided that

what came next was a bit of a long story. In fact, it was probably a good idea to leave out the bit in the middle about being embarrassingly naive during a chase, not to mention the whole sorry episode with Marcella the Pirate and her gang. 'They caught up with me.'

'And?'

'They found the box and got the wrong idea about what I'd nicked. There was a bit of argy-bargy, and then we sorted it all out and went our separate ways,' said The Pan. What a giant lie. Oh well, it was kind of what happened, if you didn't look at the details too closely.

There was a squeaking sound from Frank's leather trench coat as he shifted position. Clearly he wasn't buying it.

'Who done that then?' asked Big Merv pointing an accusing finger at The Pan's bruised nose and grazed face. 'And how d'you get that bleedin' thumbprint on my nice white pristine card?'

'Well, the conversation did get quite heated at one point. But most of this,' The Pan pointed to his face, 'was because I was a bit nervous afterwards and I fell down some stairs.'

'Yeh. I bet you walked into a door an' all,' growled Big Merv. He heaved an irritable sigh but said nothing more. As the silence lengthened and The Big Thing looked long and hard at him, The Pan prayed his story had stuck. Big Merv's antennae were waving backwards and forwards, a sign of thought, but that didn't necessarily mean he was thinking good things. Eventually, after what felt like an eternity, Big Merv spoke. 'Alright,' he said and he nodded at Frank who strode out of the room, pausing only to give The Pan a contemptuous look. Still nothing was said and The Pan fidgeted nervously. He could feel the cold sweat starting round his temples and the back of his neck again, not to mention a certain dampness about the armpits. He didn't dare look round when he heard the door, behind him, open and close softly.

'We're ready, Boss.' Harry this time.

'Sweet.' Big Merv stood up and addressed The Pan. 'You ain't got nothing more to tell me?'

He nearly caved and told Big Merv everything. But then he convinced himself that it was very much better if his boss didn't know about Marcella the Pirate. It was bad enough having to try and get away with the story he was telling, but he didn't want to drag Fred 'Fingers' Davies into it. Or worse, have some kind of gang war started on his account. It was bound to get ugly, and Marcella would find out who'd ratted on her. The Pan decided that there were enough folks trying to kill him without adding someone as dangerous and clearly psychopathic as her to the list.

'You hear what I asked?'

'Yes, sorry, and no, that's all I can say.'

Big Merv heaved a sigh. 'All you can say. Yer, see, that right there, son, is my problem. Coz I reckon it ain't the whole story.' Big Merv nodded and The Pan felt the weight of a heavy hand on his shoulder. Uh oh, this wasn't good. 'Alright, then you gotta come with me.' Big Merv stood up and walked to the door.

'On yer feet, you little scrote,' snapped Harry.

Chapter 9
The final curtain

With a growing sense of trepidation The Pan followed Big Merv downstairs to the club's kitchen. The whole way, he could feel the presence of Smasher Harry behind him. And he was pretty sure the two enforcers from the hall had joined the party too. His suspicions were confirmed when one of them ducked past him and opened the door for Big Merv. The group trooped into the kitchen, through the preparation area to the cool storage units at the back. One was a deep freezer and one was a giant walk-in fridge. It was the fridge Big Merv walked into. It was larger than The Pan expected but that wasn't the first thing he noticed—what struck him at once was the sight of Finicky Bert, the jeweller from whom he'd collected the box. The poor old boy was hanging, upside down, trussed up like a chicken with his arms pinned to his side. Beside him, wearing what The Pan thought was an unnecessarily smug expression, stood Frank the Knife. 'Arnold,' whispered The Pan.

He understood that any attempt on his part to gloss over the unfortunate events surrounding his most recent delivery would have consequences, but he hadn't envisaged anything like this. He felt sick, his legs were wobbly and his head was beginning to spin. He put one hand out clutching for something, anything, that he could use for support. But there wasn't anything nearby. His vision tunnelled and he sank to his knees.

'Get 'im upright,' said Big Merv. Frank darted forward, Harry stepped up from behind and, taking an arm apiece, they dragged The Pan into a standing position. He looked up, because Big Merv was taller than he was; a lot taller. He noticed that The Big Thing's antennae were sticking straight up, as if they were statically charged, a sure sign of anger. Arnold's trousers, this wasn't good.

'Have I got your attention now, you little squirt?' asked Big Merv. His voice had a dangerously quiet, threatening edge.

The Pan wasn't sure whether or not the question was rhetorical but decided it was probably best to answer it anyway. 'Yes, sir,' he squeaked.

'Good. I reckon you know Finicky Bert, the jeweller what you collected Ms Myrtle's present from. I would let you shake hands but Bert's kinda tied up right now.' The Pan gulped. 'Say hello to the little scrote, Bert.'

'Mmm mmm,' said Finicky Bert. The Pan thought it might have been 'hello' but as he was wearing a gag it was difficult to tell. He didn't look as if he was injured—in fact, he didn't even seem that perturbed, but that might just be bravado. However cucumber calm he appeared to be mentally, hanging upside down was obviously having some physical effects. As The Pan took in his bulging eyes and bright red face, he wondered how long the poor man had been hanging there.

'Hello,' squeaked The Pan in a small voice.

'Now we're down here, I wanna confirm what you said. You reckon that the box what you delivered is the one Finicky Bert, here, gave you.'

'Um—'

'Yeh?'

'I ran into—'

'A spot of bother. Yeh. I got that, pal. What I ain't clear about is what went down.'

'Please, please don't kill me ... or Bert I—'

'Shut it. I ain't done talking. See, the jewels you was supposed to pick up wasn't as expensive as the ones what you delivered. And d'you know what pal? Finicky Bert reckons he made that necklace you delivered a couple a months ago, for someone else. Ain't that right, Bert?'

'Mmm,' Bert confirmed and nodded. The movement caused him to swing about a bit. Big Merv put a hand out and steadied him so he hung still again. 'Mmmks,' said Bert.

'Pleasure, mate,' said Big Merv with absolutely no warmth whatsoever. He turned to face The Pan. 'That means I got me a conundrum,' he took a step closer.

'You have?' asked The Pan weakly. He tried to move backwards but Frank and Harry held him still.

'Yer. See, Ms Myrtle, she's proper classy, but she ain't gonna be around forever. I can see the signs. She's got a good heart an' that but I reckon she's gonna end it soon.'

'You can't let her kill herself, she has a kid,' blurted The Pan.

Big Merv's eyes bulged and he looked as if he was about to explode. 'Arnold's cobblers! She ain't gonna kill 'erself, you total numpty! What you got between them ears? Mush? I meant she's got 'er eye on some other geezer, an' before long, she's gonna have "the talk", an' she's gonna be history.'

'You mean you're going to kill her?' croaked The Pan. He was so petrified he could hardly speak.

'NO! You pranny! Effin' Arnold!' Big Merv shook his head in exasperation at The Pan's stupidity. 'I mean that she an' I ain't gonna be an item. By The Prophet's arse! Don't make me spell this out, son. I got pride.'

'Sorry.'

'You'd better be,' said Big Merv and he resumed his story. 'I wanna carry on treatin' her right, but at the same time I don't wanna break the bank neither. Not when I'm on a losing run, you get me?'

'Ah ... yes, I think I do,' said The Pan.

'Arnold's cobblers! It's about smeckin' time! So this is

where it gets tricky, see? Coz Bert swears he gave you a lovely pair of earrings, what he'd made special; nothing fancy, just paste an' that but they looked the pukka job. An' you're sayin' he gave you one of the classiest bespoke jobs he ever done. Now, I reckoned Bert here coulda been lyin'. An' I don't like it when people lie to me, so we had a chat.'

'Yes,' said The Pan with a fearful glance at Bert hanging, upside down from the ceiling. 'I can see that.'

'Yer,' Big Merv stepped closer and again The Pan tried, to no avail, to move backwards as Frank and Harry held him fast. 'An' that means we got a problem. Coz what you're tellin' me ain't right, an' guess what? Them earrings have miraculously turned up in Bert's shop, just like you thought. Now, we know you got street skills, son. You can dip folks but I reckon you ain't that good. So what I wanna know is this,' he jabbed The Pan in the chest with one finger between each word, 'what the smeck you done an' who done it with you?'

The Pan's throat was dry and when he tried to swallow his tongue stuck to the roof of his mouth. 'I—' he began.

'Yer?' growled Big Merv. The Pan tried to speak again but all that came out was a fearful croak. 'I can't 'ear you mate. All I wanna know is what you done. Or is Bert lyin'? Have I gotta hurt Bert to get the truth, son?'

Finally, The Pan managed to speak. 'No,' he said, except his voice was hardly more than a whisper. 'Please don't hurt Bert, Big Merv, sir.'

Big Merv leaned down and put his face close to The Pan's. 'Who've I gotta hurt instead, pal?'

The Pan was on the verge of crying. He closed his eyes and blinked back the tears. 'No-one, I hope,' he whispered.

'Looks like I gotta hurt someone,' said Big Merv, 'and it looks like it's gonna be you. Unless,' he left the word hanging for a moment, 'you can tell me different. You tell me what happened, an' if I reckon you're bein' straight with me, we might all be friends again.'

The Pan's stomach turned over. He looked past the sinister bulk of his incandescent boss, to the upside-down face of Bert, and their eyes met. Almost imperceptibly, Bert gave an encouraging nod. He was the only one in the room who didn't seem to be angry with The Pan. Indeed, considering that he was hanging upside down by his feet, he didn't seem to be particularly worried at all. Then again, for all the bulging eyes and red face, he had been a trapeze artist. Maybe he was used to hanging upside down. He was also a skilled jeweller which probably meant that whatever Big Merv did to him, he was too valuable to actually murder.

'OK,' said The Pan, and he told Big Merv what happened, how he'd been an idiot, got caught in a trap and been rolled over by some gangster called Marcella.

Big Merv stood and listened with his arms folded, which served to make him look even more big and intimidating. He appeared casual but The Pan could see that he was far from it—his antennae were moving slowly as he thought and, at one point, statically charged as his rage returned for a few moments. When The Pan described how the two groups had started fighting one another, Big Merv chuckled. It wasn't exactly a humorous chuckle but it kindled a small ember of hope in The Pan that he might escape from this, and Finicky Bert with him.

'That's a whole heap of trouble,' Big Merv said when The Pan's story was told, nodding in apparent approval. 'You done alright to get outta that, sunshine,' he said.

'Thank you,' said The Pan. Because it was always worth being polite to other beings, especially when they're really scary and you're trying to convince them not to murder you.

'So, I gotta get this straight. You gave that little bleeder

Marcella the slip (nice move there, mate) but you still ain't got the box off of her.'

'Someone gave me the other box.'

Big Merv laughed. 'That's funny, right boys?' Either side of The Pan, holding him by his arms, Frank and Harry laughed dutifully, with the standard zero percent actual mirth. 'He's a joker, this bloke,' growled Big Merv grabbing The Pan by his collar and yanking him forward so they were nose to nose. Frank and Harry had to stagger a bit to keep hold of him. 'Listen son. There's a lotta blokes what think I should drop you in the River Dang with concrete boots on.'

'Yer,' agreed Frank.

'Please—' began The Pan.

'I don't wanna do that,' said Big Merv, speaking over him. 'Coz I reckon you got potential. But my patience ain't infinite, sunshine, and you're taking a smeckin' lotta trainin'. I'm givin' you a lot more slack than I'd give most blokes already.'

Arnold's socks! This was a lot of slack? What was playing hardball like? 'Please, Big Merv sir, please don't hurt me!' The Pan whimpered. Pathetic.

'Then don't yank my chain, you little bleeder.' Big Merv let go of The Pan's collar and pushed him backwards. He staggered into Harry, who pushed him upright. 'If you wanna see tomorrow, you're gonna be straight with me an' the boys here, ain'tcha?'

'It's a guy I've known a long time,' said The Pan. OK, so technically, it wasn't a long time—it had only been a few weeks since The Pan first went to The Parrot and Screwdriver. But he felt as if he'd known the friends he'd met there for much longer. Not that Fred was a friend exactly but ... The Pan suddenly noticed the way Big Merv was staring at him, with an expectant expression. Arnold's bogies, he'd lost the thread. Where had he got to? Oh yeh.

'This guy picks pockets,' he said.

'Yer?'

'Yeh, and he stole the necklace from a Grongle. He was in the crowd when Marcella took the earrings and well ... to be honest, I think he took them from her.'

Big Merv raised his eyebrows. 'This thieving mate of yours, who does he work for?'

'He's freelance.'

'Yeh?' To The Pan, Big Merv's tone sounded sinister.

'Yes.'

'Why didn'tcha just deliver the earrings?'

'Because he wouldn't give them to me. I think he meant to but he had a look at them first, and he saw they weren't real and he gave me something else instead, in case— in case—'

'In case what, sunshine?'

'In case you discovered they weren't real and they were meant to be and Bert was pulling a fast one. Sorry Bert, you didn't strike me as the type but—'

'Mmm m-mmm,' said the old fellow which The Pan took to be 'That's alright.'

'Thanks,' said The Pan to Bert before addressing Big Merv again. 'I asked him for the earrings but he wasn't having it. And the necklace was better than not delivering anything.' The Pan realised how fast he was speaking and stopped.

There was a long, long, pause. The Pan took a deep breath. Rivers of cold sweat were running down his neck and from his temples; worse, it was also running into his eyes. It stung and he wished Frank and Harry weren't holding his arms so tightly. He tried to wipe his face on his shoulder.

At last, Big Merv spoke. 'If Mr Gaspot an' Bert 'ere are right about that necklace, your mate shoulda sold it an' retired.'

'He said it was too distinctive, too good, too difficult to sell.'

'Mo. Mff mmm mmm fmaff grkably ooking ger f̄,' said Finicky Bert through his gag.

'Eh?' asked Big Merv.

Frank, who was clearly more used to conversing with gagged beings translated. 'He reckons no, coz the Grongles are probably looking for it.'

'Fair point, Bert. So you're sayin' he couldn't sell it?' said Big Merv.

'Hmmect,' Bert confirmed.

Big Merv turned his attention back to The Pan. 'Has he got a name, this bloke?'

The Pan swallowed. 'Not that I know of.'

'He's your mate an' you don't know 'is name?'

'Yes, please believe me. I know it sounds strange, but I can't tell you his name,' said The Pan.

Something in Big Merv's eyes changed at that. The trouble was, The Pan wasn't sure if it was a good change or a bad one. 'He got a nickname?'

'Thieving John,' said The Pan promptly. Arnold no, don't lie, you'll never remember what you said! Never mind, too late now.

Big Merv nodded. 'Alright lads,' he said. Smasher Harry and Frank the Knife released The Pan's arms with what was clearly a considerable amount of disappointment. 'Harry, he done the delivery, so I'm gonna give 'im the cash an' you're gonna show 'im out.'

'Aren't you gonna chuck 'im—'

'Nah. Not this time. Ms Myrtle's happy enough with that necklace and it ain't cost me nothing.' He swung round suddenly and stepped up to The Pan. 'But if you ever, ever lie to me again you snotty little Herbert, I ain't gonna be playing Mr Nice Guy no more. You get me?'

Mr Nice Guy? Holy Arnold! That was Mr Nice Guy?
'Yes sir,' squeaked The Pan.

'Good,' Big Merv pulled an envelope from his jacket pocket and shoved at The Pan. 'Here.'

'W— What's this?' stammered The Pan.

'You done the delivery, so you get paid. Now get outta my sight before I change my mind.'

The Pan fumbled the envelope into his own pocket. He was shaking so much that walking was a challenge, but he managed to follow Harry swiftly back out onto the street.

****

As soon as The Pan had gone, Big Merv turned to Frank and the other heavies. 'Get 'im down,' he said pointing to where the jeweller hung from the ceiling. 'C'mon, look lively lads! He's gone a funny colour.'

'Yes, Boss,' said Frank.

'Mmm momemy mmm mn,' said Finicky Bert. 'I'm quite alright,' he added as Frank removed the gag.

'You don't look it,' said Big Merv. 'Hurry it up lads.' He watched with a critical eye as Frank and one of the others unhooked Finicky Bert from the ceiling with the help of the other two heavies and put him the right way up. 'You sure you're alright there, mate?' Big Merv asked as Frank undid the rope binding him up.

'Perfectly, thank you.' Bert smoothed his remaining hair with a shaky hand.

'You certain. I got brandy?'

'No, thank you.'

'Sorry Bert mate, I gotta thank you. You done me a proper favour there. I owe you big time.'

'Ah, it was nothing.'

Big Merv scratched his head. His antennae tied themselves into a knot and slowly unknotted. 'That little scrote took longer to crack than I thought.'

76

'Heavens, isn't that the truth! I thought that was going to take forever. Is he always like that?' asked Bert.

'Yer, 's like gettin' blood out a bleedin' rock. Why the snotty nosed little Herbert can't be straight I dunno.'

Finicky Bert raised a finger as if he was about to say something like, 'maybe he's petrified of you', but then clearly thought better of it.

'Course, he's loyal enough. Dead tricky to catch an' all,' said Big Merv.

'He's a natural clown.'

'On yer circus scale.'

'On my circus scale.'

'Yer, I gotta hand it to 'im, the lad's a quick thinker,' agreed Big Merv and then he began to laugh. 'Thieving John, my arse!' he guffawed. 'There's only one bloke in town who coulda done that.'

'Fred "Fingers" Davies,' said Bert.

'S'right.'

'You want us to bash 'im?' asked Frank.

'What for, you plank?' Big Merv retorted. 'Fred's alright, no-one's come to no 'arm, an' I got confirmation that that jumped-up little squirt Marcella the Pirate thinks she can do what she likes. Sounds like that one's gettin' above her station.'

'We gonna ice 'er Boss?'

With a quick glance at Finicky Bert, Big Merv said quietly, 'We'll talk about that later Frank, when Harry comes back. Bert, you gonna be alright, sunshine?'

'Of course. After all those years on the trapeze, a few minutes hanging upside down is a walk in the park.'

Big Merv wasn't wholly convinced. 'You reckon?'

'Oh yes.'

'Sweet,' he said, clapping Bert on the shoulder, making the old boy stagger a few paces forward, 'Frank, take Bert upstairs an' tell Bob to give 'im a ride home.'

'Yes, Boss,' said Frank.

'Tell 'er to give 'im a bottle of brandy an' all.'

'Yes, Boss.'

'An' Bert,' Big Merv took a brown envelope from the inside pocket of his jacket. It was a great deal more bulky than the one he'd given The Pan. He held it out. 'Thanks pal. Here's something for your trouble.'

'Oh no, I really—'

'Take it,' said Big Merv in a tone of voice that implied it was definitely an order. Bert didn't argue.

The end

Other books by M T McGuire

If you'd like to find out what happens next, look out for the other books in this series:

Small Beginnings
K'Barthan Shorts, Hamgeean Misfit: No 1
When your very existence is treason, employment opportunities are thin on the ground. But when one of the biggest crime lords in the city makes The Pan of Hamgee a job offer he can't refuse, it's hard to tell what the dumbest move is; accepting the offer or saying, no to Big Merv. Neither will do much for The Pan's life expectancy.

Nothing To See Here
K'Barthan Shorts, Hamgeean Misfit: No 2
It's midwinter and preparations for the biggest religious festival in the K'Barthan year are in full swing. Yes, even though, officially, religious activity has been banned, no-one's going to ignore Arnold, The Prophet's Birthday, especially not Big Merv. He orders The Pan of Hamgee to deliver the traditional Birth of The Prophet gift to his accountants and lawyers.

As usual, The Pan has managed to elicit the unwanted attention of the security forces. Can he make the delivery and get back to the The Parrot and Screwdriver pub in time for an unofficial Prophet's Birthday celebration with his friends?

Too Good To Be True
K'Barthan Extras, Hamgeean Misfit: No 4
When The Pan of Hamgee encounters some mudlarkers trying to land a box on the banks of the River Dang he is happy to help. Having accepted a share of the contents as a reward he cannot believe his luck. It contains one of the most expensive delicacies available in K'Barth; Goojan spiced sausage. If he can sell it, the sausage might spell the end of his troubles, but knowing his luck it could bring a whole load more.

You can also read more about The Pan of Hamgee's adventures in K'Barth in a series of four full-length books.

The K'Barthan Series

All The Pan of Hamgee wants is a quiet life.

So why did he have to fall in love with a woman living a different version of reality, upset a murderous tyrant and then run out of places to hide?

Now all he has to do is face his inner demons, rescue everything he holds dear and save the world, or die trying.

Oh yes, and he's an abject coward.

Great. No pressure then.

Escape From B-Movie Hell

Bronze Medal winner, The Wishing Shelf Book Awards, 2015.

If you asked Andi Turbot whether she had anything in common with Flash Gordon she'd say no, emphatically. Saving the world is for dynamic, go-ahead leaders of men. And while it would be nice to see a woman getting involved for a change, she believes she could be the least well-equipped being in her galaxy for the job.

Then her best friend Eric reveals that he's an extraterrestrial. He's not just any E.T. either. He's Gamalian: seven feet tall, lobster-shaped and covered in marmite-scented goo. Just when Andi's getting used to that he tells her about the apocalypse and really ruins her day.

The human race will perish unless Eric's Gamalian superiors step in. Abducted and trapped on an alien ship, Andi must convince the Gamalians her world is worth saving. Or escape from their clutches and save it herself.

Find out more at: www.hamgee.co.uk/books.html

Author News

Never miss a new release again! Sign up for M T Mail. Just visit this link: http://www.hamgee.co.uk/freenbook

You can choose to hear about everything or just new releases. You can also keep up to date with all things M T McGuire by joining her K'Barthan Jolly Japery Facebook Group.

To join, go here: http://bit.ly/JollyJapes

Or you can follow M T McGuire on these social media:

Website: http://www.hamgee.co.uk

Blog: http://www.mtmcguire.co.uk

Twitter: @mtmcguireauthor